THE
BREACH

THE RESCHEN VALLEY SERIES – PART 2

Chrystyna Lucyk-Berger

Chrystyna Lucyk-Berger / Inktreks

Dornbirn, Austria

www.inktreks.com

For historical notes, background information, a list of characters in the series, a glossary and more information, visit www.inktreks.com/blog.

Book cover design by Ursula Hechenberger-Schwärzler (ursulahechenberger.com)

Cover models: Kathrin Meier, Marie Meier

Cover photos by Daniele Reseghetti/Shutterstock and Ursula Hechenberger-Schwärzler

The Breach, a Reschen Valley Novel (2)/ Chrystyna Lucyk-Berger. – 1st ed.

ISBN: 978-1-985723-41-2

ASIN: B0795RGKFW

Welcome (back!) to the Reschen Valley series. I am thrilled that you have chosen *this* book.

Pssst... if you haven't read the first instalment, you may want to. Though future instalments will be stand-alone, No Man's Land *(part 1) and* The Breach *(part 2) were meant to be one big book. Because of its final size, we made it into two separate titles. You may also choose to read the compilation "Reschen Valley Box Set Season 1: 1920-1924" containing the first two books and the prequel.*

Please do not forget to leave a review or rating on your favourite platforms. Thank you so much!

TO MY DADDY—

You know why. I miss you.

1922−1924

Why should we care for 180,000 Germans under Italian domination? If, as a National Socialist, I put myself in the position of Italy, I have to agree fully with that country's claim to a strategic border.

— ADOLF HITLER, QUOTED IN THE *CORRIERE ITALIANO*, OCTOBER 1922

CONTENTS

ARLUND, NOVEMBER 1922

At the cemetery on St. Anna's hill, Katharina stood with Annamarie's hand in hers. She pointed out her two great-uncles and Annamarie's great-grandmother.

At the engraved photo of her parents, Katharina said, "Annamarie, that was your Opa, Josef Thaler. And this was your Oma, Marianna Thaler. They were my mother and father, just like I am your mama and Papa is—"

Katharina could try all she wanted, but Annamarie was Angelo Grimani's. Her daughter had his long fingers, his eyes, his slight dimple on her chin, and even a shade of his Italian colouring. Everyone in the valley said that Annamarie looked like Katharina. Even Jutta and Florian, the only two who knew Annamarie was Angelo's, said with careful diplomacy that Annamarie would be tall like her mama, and a beauty like her too.

Maybe. But Katharina saw her daughter's other half just as prominently.

Annamarie slipped to the ground and grabbed at the black-eyed Susans on the graves, and Katharina bent to rescue the flowers, but a sharp pain in her back halted her, and Annamarie had the first daisy's head off in no time. Katharina stretched, one hand on her rounded belly: her next child, Florian's. Before her daughter could get hold of another flower, Katharina scooped her up and winced at the strain of it. Annamarie was what weighed on her most. It would be the father's side of the child's story Katharina would never be able to properly share.

She remembered how, when Florian received news of his mother's death the month before, he'd slowly folded the telegram and said, "I'm sorry my mother never got to meet her granddaughter." His voice had faltered at the end, and he looked at Katharina's belly. "Or maybe it will be a boy."

When she had Annamarie wrapped and tied to her back again, Katharina called for the dog. Hund loped up the path back to Arlund, turning sideways to stop and check on their progress. Before entering the woods, Katharina looked down into the valley at the skeletons of new barracks between Reschen and Graun. The area for the Italian officials was growing, the buildings becoming sturdier, more permanent. In the last two years, the wives and children of the border guards and police had joined their husbands. There was a new schoolteacher from farther down in Italy. And Captain Rioba was now prefect, which meant Georg Roeschen was no longer mayor of Graun. Jutta had complained, with a sour face, about how the landscape was changing, and Kaspar Ritsch had said that if the Italians were building so much, then chances were that the Etsch River wouldn't be diverted to where the *Walscher*—the Italians—were living.

"Then we should all relocate to the Italian quarter," Opa had retorted.

Katharina reached the wayward cross and put a few daisies into the vase at Christ's feet. Above them, she heard the cry of a goshawk. It grasped something in its claws, but she could not make out what. It was a fine day for the first of November, warm and sunny, and the mountain peaks were not even covered in snow yet. She crossed the bridge at the Karlinbach and came to the clearing leading to Arlund. In the distance, smoke curled from the chimney of the Thalerhof. She smiled at the thought of surprising Florian with the hare she'd caught in one of their traps. She would bake it in the Roman clay pot with cabbage and a thick sauce, the way he liked it.

At the sound of running water in the *Hof*, Hund dashed for the fountain set just before the house on the garden side. That summer, Florian and Opa had carved out a fresh log, hollowing it out first, then tapping into the spring below with a wooden spigot where the water ran through the small plug at the bottom of the log, nonstop. When it was very hot, the dog would jump in and crouch to her midriff, lapping up the water as if she'd just crossed a desert. But now Hund just stood on her hind legs to drink, and Katharina untied Annamarie from her.

The girl awoke and began fussing, then grabbed the crucifix hanging around Katharina's neck. After she set the child down, Katharina went to the fountain and splashed cool water on her face. At the sight of the window boxes, she realised she'd forgotten to water the geraniums, which were wilting in the unseasonable heat.

With a bucket in hand and a blanket in the other, Opa came out of the workshop. His cough had returned, rattling within him like loosened gravel rolling down a slope.

"I've pulled some of the softer apples out," he said when he caught his breath again. "They won't make the winter. Thought you'd make a cake tonight."

"That, and something for your chest." She pulled the pouch away from her side and held up the hare. "I've got something too."

He glanced at her middle. "Your husband should be doing that kind of work, not you. Gives him a feeling of self-worth, a tie to the land."

"Now, Opa," she started, but he walked away, muttering that he was going to Graun.

"Been two weeks since anyone's picked up the post," he tossed over his shoulder.

She would go, she wanted to say, but voices from behind the house stopped her from calling after him. Florian appeared with Toni Ritsch. She hung up the hare before greeting Toni and asking about Patricia.

"She's fine," Toni said. "The baby is keeping her busy. Spirited boy. We've named him Andreas."

"A fine name. Tell her I'll stop in tomorrow and help her."

"We're negotiating the bull," Florian said. Though he smiled, he gave her a look that signalled he was not pleased about the business.

Toni rubbed his beard and nodded at the hare. "Looks like dinner. I should make my way home."

"Nonsense. It's early," Florian said. "Come in and have some refreshment."

"I won't change the conditions," Toni said. He turned to Katharina. "Florian's showing me new ways to earn money. Told me about his mother's house in Nuremberg and the rent he's earning from it. It's a good idea. Think I'll do something similar. We Ritsches have lots of property, and we could build something to lease out. Maybe even to some Italians. It's time I got something back from them. I'll show them what *bauernschlau* means."

Katharina glanced at Annamarie. Nobody—not even Florian —knew her daughter's real ethnic background, and the way people talked about the Italians, she would do anything to keep it that way.

"And the terms of your bull have now changed?" she said. "Is that why you two are still negotiating?"

Toni at least had the decency to look sheepish. "It's the economy—"

"Indeed, Toni. Just that. And loyalty. My grandfather and your father go a long way back. There are certainly some things that have not been squared away over the years." She knew about how Opa had lent the Ritsches money when Kaspar had fallen on bad times, and Opa had never asked for a single *Heller* back. "We're not Italians either, Toni. We're your neighbours. Remember that as you negotiate."

Florian clapped Toni on the shoulder. "Let's go in and have a glass. We'll just talk, and then you can think about it."

Katharina watched the men go into the house, remembering how Toni and his friends had once forced her and the other schoolgirls to climb the Planggers' tree so that they could look up their dresses. Patricia had refused to do it, and Toni had pinned her down on the ground. Their saving grace had been the call of a farmer looking for one of his sons.

"Florian," she called after them, "where's my father's knife? I need to dress the hare."

Her husband returned to her and lowered his voice. "You want to tell me about those dues owed now?"

"I'll tell you what kind of a neighbour you're dealing with," she whispered. Just the least of the worst. "A few years before my mother passed away, we used to have hares in the hutches out back. My mother went to feed them one day and found one that had died, of old age, we supposed. She buried it out in the meadow somewhere.

"Toni's dog dug it up and left it on the Ritsches' front stoop as a gift. When Toni found that hare, he brushed it off, got it as clean as he could, and went and put that dead animal back into the hutch, like nothing happened."

"No," Florian said, eyes wide, clearly stifling a laugh out of respect. "Tell me he didn't."

Katharina nodded. "My mother, bless her soul, went out to feed those hares the next morning. When she saw the one that had returned from the grave, her heart dropped into her pants. We all came running at her screams."

Florian coughed into his collar, his shoulders shaking, and Katharina felt a laugh rising in her as well.

"Did he ever admit it?" he asked.

"Kaspar had to."

He sucked in a deep breath, trying to put on a straight face. "I understand."

"Now you know what kind of people he is."

He held out her papa's knife to her. "You'll tell me the other things later."

"Oh, I certainly will."

She took the handle and started to dress the hare.

Toni and Florian were still discussing cattle and properties in the sitting room when Opa returned from Graun. Katharina folded the apples into the cake batter as he greeted Toni first, and then, as a way to apologise for his earlier brash comments, she supposed, Opa said something about the delicious smells from the baking hare before handing her a small package.

"This came for you."

It was the size of a book and posted from Bolzano. Katharina knew what it was but pretended to be surprised.

"Well, open it."

"When I'm done with the cake."

He cupped a fist to his mouth and coughed again. She touched his arm.

"Next time," she said, "you send Florian or me into town for your papers and post. With winter coming, you need to get that cough under control."

Opa patted Annamarie's head as she played amongst the scattered pots and pans. Katharina watched him wander into the sitting room, organise the stacks of newspapers, clamp his empty pipe between his teeth, and unfold his first paper, the back page for the farmers' news first.

She poured the cake into the tin, popped it into the oven, and discreetly unwrapped her package.

It was her Italian primer. She leafed through the pages, holding the book close to her middle, and mouthed the conjugations for the verbs *read* and *write*.

She heard Toni say he had to leave, but when Florian came up behind her, Katharina nearly jumped out of her skin.

He reached for the book. "What's this?"

"Don't tell Opa," she whispered. "He won't have it." She showed him the primer.

Her husband looked unconvinced. "You had better put it where he won't find it."

Toni was at the door when Opa slammed his newspaper into his lap, face flushed.

"Look at this." He jabbed at the front page with his pipe. "The Fascists are positioned in the Po plains."

"When did this happen?" Toni strode over to Opa and stood over his shoulder.

Opa looked at the top of the newspaper. "October twenty-fourth."

Florian asked for the paper and read aloud. "At a Fascist Congress in Naples, Mussolini was quoted as saying, 'Our program is simple: we want to rule Italy.'"

"And this one," Opa complained, raising another issue, also on the front page. "The twenty-ninth."

Florian scanned the article, and Katharina placed the Italian primer on the corner of the counter, intending to go to him, but he lowered the paper before she reached him.

"Forget about the Po for a moment," her husband said to Opa and Toni. "There are twenty thousand Blackshirts marching in Rome right now. The prime minister ordered a state of siege, but the king's refused to sign a military order."

"What does that mean?" Katharina asked.

Her husband faced Opa, as if he'd asked the question. "It means the king will give Mussolini whatever he wants."

Toni came around from Opa's chair and put his hands on his waist, his anger taking up the middle of the room. "To hell if I'm going to be called Antonio from now on. Should've stayed up on the alp, that's what. Crossed the border as soon as I could have."

"Good thing I'm still a German citizen," Florian scoffed.

Opa looked bewildered. "What good is that to you now? You going to pick up this house, the barn, and all the cattle and move them across the border, or what?"

Katharina groaned softly. *Don't give him any ideas.* Her husband had not been able to hide his growing admiration for the nationalists in Germany.

"If the Fascists take over Italy," Toni said, "the first thing they'll do is make that Ettore Tolomei head of something and make sure all of our rights are signed out of law."

"I won't have it," Opa yelled. "I won't have Tyrol taken over by thugs."

Florian turned to Toni. "What do we do then?"

"Fight." Toni wagged his hat at Opa. "Johannes, it's time we start that resistance."

Opa stood up. "I'll back you and anyone else who wants to take a stand."

Florian bit his bottom lip, a gesture Katharina recognised as her own when in duress.

"I'll talk to the boys." Toni nodded. "We'll get ourselves organised. Florian?"

Katharina turned away, closing her ears to the nonsense. There would be no resistance. Father Wilhelm or Jutta would talk them all out of it. Against the two of them, the "boys," as Toni had called them—she cringed when Opa coughed again—would get a scolding, that was all.

She picked up the cake bowl to wash it out and inadvertently knocked the primer she'd lain on the table. It fell to the ground, and before she could bend over to pick it up, Toni had already scooped it up and held it out to her, until his gaze fell on the cover. When he pulled the primer away from her reach, she noted the grim look on his face. Her blood froze, and as he leaned in, he was so close she could smell the wine on his breath.

"You remember whose land you're on?" he whispered.

Katharina's heart banged against her ribs. She recalled how he'd pinned Patricia to the ground. She stared at the book in his hand, and she could feel his breath on her neck.

"Hmmm? That you're not one of us has always been clear with your mother's mixed blood. Something Slavic, wasn't she? Polish? They ain't got a lick of loyalty to them. Shows in how they govern their country, foreign kings and all."

"I'm as Tyrolean as any of you," Katharina choked out.

"Yeah?" He tipped his head towards the book in his hand and pressed the upper corner into her waist. "Seems you've forgotten. Married an outsider. None of us were any good for ya?" He sniffed, checked over his shoulder.

Behind him, Opa and Florian were still arguing about what form a resistance could take.

Toni finally moved away from her, but he wasn't finished. He pretended to examine the empty cake bowl, and spoke softly.

"Shame on you, Katharina. Feel sorry for your Opa here. Only people he's got left is a strange tall girl and a German. Both half-Tyroleans and ain't got no respect for tradition and what this country's gone through to get the freedom it once had."

"I didn't forget any of that." Katharina found courage in her growing outrage.

He smirked and rubbed along the edge of the bowl, her sweet cake batter gathering on the rim of his index finger.

"Good thing you're not getting this farm, Katharina. What did you think you were going to do with it as a spinster? Huh? Just wouldn't have been right."

He licked his finger before turning his back on her.

If the Thalerhof were hers—like it should be—she'd march to the barn right now, fetch Opa's rifle out of its hiding place, and chase Toni all the way into the valley and across the border herself.

Toni was addressing the men again. "You throw your hat in with us, Johannes, and we'll get a resistance going, but you make good and sure you know who's in the fight with you."

At the door, he pressed his hat on his head, buzzard feather quivering, before facing Florian. "Many thanks for the wine, but my terms for the bull haven't changed. Take it or leave it."

2

BOLZANO, NOVEMBER 1922

On their way back from Castel Roncolo, Angelo walked with Marco and Chiara along the Talvera River. Below the promenade, the current swept branches and twigs, fallen leaves, and someone's handkerchief southwards, a late-autumn migration. To their left, the vineyards were already stripped of their fruit. Between the Bolzano hills, the chimneys of the Rosengarten range rose dusty and brown with just the slightest glaze of snow.

Chiara stopped and gazed at Castel Roncolo behind them. "It's rather imposing, is it not?"

Angelo liked it. It had flair. "I find it elegant, even Italian-like."

"I heard that the family turned it into their summer residence in the fourteenth century." She leaned into him, and her hair caught the November sunlight and blended with the tones of her russet dress.

Having her like this gave him pleasure, something rare between them these days. In his other arm, he pressed Marco to him, who giggled and took Angelo's face into both his hands and gave him a clumsy kiss. His soft black curls tickled, and Angelo brought Marco's head closer to kiss him back.

Chiara looked back at the palace while stroking the boy's leg. "I suppose there is something gay about it. Maybe the castle's taken on the spirit of its function, as a holiday residence, that is. If you believe in spirits, that is."

"I believe in good engineering." He held his arm out for her.

They moved along the river, and he wanted to take off his coat the way Chiara had her feathered cape. It lay in Marco's otherwise empty pram, the ecru and black feathers making it look as if they were harbouring an exotic swan. He set his son onto the gravel path, and Marco beelined into the field. The air was crisp with the scents of autumn. The chestnut trees had dropped their fanlike leaves, and Marco toddled through them, trying to kick them up as he had seen his father do earlier. Angelo chased after him, caught him, and whipped him into the air, raising his son high. The bare tree branches stretched out like a web behind Marco. When Angelo looked back at his wife, she was smiling in a way he had not seen in a long time. Too long. November was the skeleton ready to be shrouded by winter, but Chiara looked like the splendour of October. He wanted to talk to her again about a brother or sister for Marco. He wanted to close the divide between them and be intimate with his wife again.

Returning to her, he saw Chiara was already pointing the pram for home. Angelo grew tense. Here in the park, he was just a man spending time with his wife and son. As soon as they headed for the villa, he'd slip into a world over which he had no control, a world where he and Chiara fought in relative silence. He kept his association with the Blackshirts from her, which was easy, for she was always engrossed in her newspapers and letters. Since the Bolzano Fair and the Tyrolean fatalities, political tensions had grown worse. Much worse. There had been quite the public outcry from the Tyroleans, but the Fascists who now occupied the Alto Adige quickly quashed any revolts. Violence erupted often, and after an attack on him by a mob of

Blackshirts, Count Edmond was now in exile. With Mussolini ruling from Rome, Chiara's letters of protest were dangerous, and a layer of fear infused the house. Except today. Today they had succeeded in leaving it all behind.

"We should have brought a picnic," he said.

"I hadn't thought it would be so warm."

"I could go back and ask the cook to put something together."

She seemed to think about it, and he let her, stopping to gaze at the castle once more. He wanted to stay here with his family and find something that would keep them together. It would take more than a picnic, but that might be the beginning. He turned back to persuade her, but Marco was in the pram, and Chiara had the swanlike cape over her shoulders, pushing for home.

A steady drip of rain on the windowpanes interrupted Angelo's reading, and he checked his office clock. Noon. The outing with Chiara and Marco the day before seemed years ago now that the weather had turned.

He rubbed his eyes. After lunch he would have to take a nap before coming back to the office.

He heard a door open at the far end of the hallway, and footsteps paraded past his office. Someone knocked at what must have been Pietro's door. Angelo turned back to the structural report he'd been reading on the Gleno Dam and hoped their lunch break would not be delayed. He'd reached the last page when the door opened and closed again, followed by the footsteps once more. The party stopped outside of Angelo's office and spoke with hushed voices before moving on. When it was silent, Angelo took his coat off the hook, glad that Pietro and he would not be too late for lunch after all.

He was setting his hat on his head, when someone knocked.

"Come in. I'm just getting ready."

Pietro's secretary. She looked upset.

"Mrs Sala?"

"They've taken the minister."

He should have gone out into the hallway. "What are the charges?"

Mrs Sala shook her head. "I wasn't able to hear them."

"Call the Villa Adige and inform my family that Minister d'Oro and I will not be home for lunch. Do not tell them why. Just say an urgent matter has come up." He had another idea. "Please call Colonel Grimani first. Tell him to meet me at the police station."

She turned to go.

"And Mrs Sala? Tell the Colonel to come immediately. His meal can wait."

He took the stairs down to the police quarters to enquire about the charges, to at least get hold of the man responsible for the case. He was surprised when the man in charge offered to let him see Pietro right away and led him to a holding room in the basement.

Pietro was standing under the window and smiled, but defeat dimmed his eyes.

"How are you?" Angelo asked.

He gestured to a chair. "They plan to only question me. I haven't been arrested yet. I imagine they could charge me with anything as little as abusing my power and manipulating bids to as much as treason. Any of it, of course, quite incorrect."

"I've called for the Colonel."

"Ah."

"You could have just retired when they asked you to, the way the Colonel advised you."

"He warned me, Angelo—he did not advise. I do not take warmly to warnings."

"You wonder where Chiara gets her fighting spirit." They both grinned, and Angelo relaxed a little. "They won't prosecute you."

"No, Angelo, if I go quietly, they will install you as minister. And you will take over quietly."

Angelo wanted to say something positive. Instead, he felt angry. "You fed too long on the successes of the German League. Count Edmond promised you too much when he promised to fight for your position. If the Tyroleans had gained control, even then there would have been nothing he could have done for you. They are just as anti-Italian as we are against the…"

"See? Violence begets violence." Pietro's smile turned from knowing to apologetic. "You must admit it was all rather exciting. The League made much progress. We believed we were running to win the race. Basic human rights. Bilingual access to all minority groups. The Tyroleans demanded only that, and yet they deserve more."

"Yes," Angelo said sharply, "and the Fascists crushed them. Even the count is in exile. You should have stopped it all then."

"I'm sorry that I convinced Edmond to flee," Pietro said.

"Why? The League was disbanded. The Fascists beat him up in the street, in broad daylight. There's nothing for him to do here now. And the countess, well, Susi should have gone with him. I don't understand why she decided to stay behind."

"Because it's her country."

Angelo gritted his teeth. "It's Italy now."

Pietro cocked his head. "It must be difficult for you, son, to be trapped in the middle of us all. Chiara. Me. Nicolo. Don't look at me that way. I know where you've been all those nights and weekends, at your father's side. I could try and explain this all to Chiara, but she is absolutely unforgiving about such things. You know she values honesty and justice and righteousness above all else. Yet I suspect that she loves you enough to protect herself. She swats away the rumours about your activity in the Fascist party because it's easier that way."

"Chiara's the main reason I'm active. To protect her."

Pietro shrugged. "You mean should her political activities—

the causes she so passionately believes in—create trouble for her? Or make it uncomfortable for you?"

Angelo looked down at his lap. "You know I don't subscribe to any of it."

"That is the danger, Angelo. The members prey on you because they believe you are weak. Do you truly believe you have the strength to take them on if you're dressed up like them?"

"Yes."

"You seem pretty certain about that."

"I wasn't before. I am now. Do you want to know the story? The one about when the Colonel handed me those orders? Then I'll tell you.

"It was on the Marmolada. My men and I were on a mission to spy on those Austro-Hungarians and the Prussians up on the peaks. This was an easy assignment for me because I've been skiing those mountains since I was a child. I know them blindfolded.

"My troops and I could get very close to their nest. We studied the enemy for weeks. We knew when they slept, we knew when they ate and what they ate, we knew when they were drunk, and we knew where and when they pissed. We even knew the lyrics to their folk songs and could have sung with them.

"Then the day came when my father, the Colonel, came on tour and began giving us orders. It was crazy, those last months of the war, Pietro. Really. There were soldiers from the navy stationed in the mountains, and fathers as commanding officers. When my father mapped out the strategy he had in mind, I saw immediately how devastating it would be to us. I sought to speak with him, but he refused to listen to me and degraded me. I know that he was under a lot of pressure. And I…" Angelo sighed. "I was afraid of him. So I put my tail between my legs, went back to my unit, and explained that we were to proceed as ordered.

"My best friend, Gasparo Farinelli, was also with me and was my first lieutenant. Before we were deployed, he asked me again to speak to the Colonel. We all knew we were being sent to a slaughter, and they thought that because he was my father... Well, when I did not go to him, Gasparo did."

Pietro shifted in his chair and inclined his head.

"I didn't realise Gasparo had gone to the Colonel," Angelo continued, "until I heard screaming coming from the officers' quarters. By the time I got there, the deed had been done. The Colonel"—Angelo cleared his throat—"punished him for insubordination. He cut out his tongue, like they do in Ethiopia. And called me a coward for sending Gasparo to him."

Pietro was mercifully quiet. When Angelo could manage again, he said, "Gasparo lived. The rest of them, I deployed according to the Colonel's orders, and the Austro-Hungarians had an easy hunting day. My men all died. I got a medal because I did not. My father had been right. I was a coward."

"I don't know if I would call you that." Pietro's voice was gentle.

"I won't be that again. You said yourself I need to keep watch over him. I'm going to do more than that. I'm going to give the orders."

His father-in-law turned to the window. "Perhaps we are much alike, you and me. We feel we must protect everyone, at a great cost to ourselves and sometimes to those we love most and are trying to protect in the first place." Pietro studied him. "If you didn't care about the projects from our department or their impacts, you would have already found your way out of this predicament of facing off against the Colonel again. Perhaps all is not lost. You will accept the nomination as the new minister, Angelo, and you will have my full support and my guidance, as promised." He shrugged, "If you accept it."

Someone knocked on the door, and a policeman led Mrs Sala in. "I did not reach the Colonel," she said. "I was told he is in Rome on business."

Angelo frowned. "In Rome? When will he be back?"

"I'm afraid I didn't ask."

"That's fine, Mrs Sala. Thank you," Pietro said.

When she left the room, he turned to Angelo. "You will begin learning how to get the things that you want and need. You tell your father that there are some conditions on which you will accept the nomination. You tell him that you want my detention to be kept quiet. Don't allow the Fascists to sensationalize this as a victory of some kind. If they try to make a spectacle of me, you will refuse the nomination."

Angelo ran a hand through his hair and stared at the ceiling.

Outside, coming from the square behind the building, was a great deal of noise and excited chatter.

"Angelo, look at me." Pietro put a hand on his shoulder. "He will not only accept these terms, he will carry your message to the party gladly. I can assure you that."

That afternoon, Angelo passed groups of people heading to the marketplace. Something was happening, but he had no time to find out about the latest commotion. When he reached the villa, the hallway was empty, but he heard voices coming from his apartments upstairs. At the parlour doors, Angelo recognised Michael Innerhofer's voice. The thought that the reporter had discovered something about Pietro's detention and beat Angelo home made him fling open the doors. Inside, scattered on the chaise longue and settees, were Chiara and Michael; Michael's brother, Peter, the now out-of-work teacher who'd been shot during the Blackshirts' raid the year before; and the countess Susi.

"Thank heavens you're home." Chiara sprang up. She rushed to Angelo, taking his hands. "Have you heard the news?"

"I was there, of course," he stammered. "But don't worry. I have everything under control. How—"

"You were in Rome?" Peter asked.

"Chiara never told us you were in Rome," Michael said.

"Of course Angelo wasn't in Rome," Susi said. "There must be some misunderstanding." She gathered the many layers of her golden gown and strode over to him, offering him her hand. "Hello, darling. So nice to see you."

Dressed in a turban, dangling earrings, and a fur cape over her dress, she was more the Egyptian queen than a European aristocrat. Both antique now.

"What's happened in Rome?" Angelo asked his wife.

The skin beneath Chiara's freckles was bright pink. "Mussolini's been made prime minister, and he's been granted dictatorial powers for one year. Angelo, a year? Parliament says he will be able to heal the country. Mussolini, to heal the country!" Her laugh sounded unnatural.

"And here, as of Wednesday," Michael said, "all correspondence with any officials are to be only in Italian. The German language is banned on all governmental levels."

"I'm sorry to hear this." Angelo referred to the latter part of the news.

Chiara pulled away from him. "Sorry to hear it? Is that all?"

What he really wanted to say was that since Mussolini's march on Rome just weeks before, he'd expected nothing but victory for the Fascists. What he wanted to say was that after the miserably irresolute and ineffectual ministers, Mussolini might finally be the man to do the job. In this crowd—these Communists—however, he was not about to start a debate. Then he remembered the discussion his father had had with Luigi Barbarasso the day Angelo eavesdropped on them. Someone had made it into Rome. An insider. He'd believed then that it had something to do with the Reschen Valley or the Gleno Dam, but they must have been discussing Benito Mussolini and his *fascisti*.

"But what news do you have, Angelo?" Susi asked.

He looked blankly at her.

"You said you were there. Where is 'there'?"

The countess never missed a thing. He turned to Chiara. "It's nothing we can't talk about later."

"Nonsense." His wife turned to the group, "We're all friends here. Why don't you all stay for lunch? Where is Father? I'll go tell him and Mama to join us. There is a lot to discuss, and he will most definitely have more to say than 'I'm sorry to hear that.'"

Chiara moved to the door, but Angelo grabbed her hand. "I need to talk to you. Alone. They can stay another time."

"You don't want our friends to stay?" Her voice was abnormally loud.

He let go of her. "Of course they can stay."

"A luncheon would be splendid," Susi said. "Wouldn't that be splendid, boys?" She slipped off her cape and perched on the edge of the divan, a bemused grin on her face. Susi was ever Chiara's ally.

In the meantime, Michael moved to a lounge chair, and Peter stayed standing, looking as if he would rather flee.

"Then I'll go inform the cook," Chiara said, but Angelo stopped her again.

"Your father's not here," he whispered. "He's been taken in for questioning."

Chiara's feigned smile vanished. "What?"

"Your father's being held…" He lowered his voice even more. "Only for the interim. I tried to reach the Colonel—"

"For God's sake, Angelo," Chiara said loudly. "Why was he arrested?" There was fear in her eyes.

"Who's been arrested?" Susi asked.

"Father," Chiara exclaimed.

Why was she making a scene?

"As soon as Nicolo returns, we will attend to it. Your father will most likely be home before tomorrow. Any charges will be dropped, Chiara," he finished gently.

"What charges, Angelo?" Her voice was steady, demanding.

Treason would be the worst. "There aren't any yet, but if there are, I promise you, they'll be dropped. For now, he's just being held for questioning."

There was a clicking sound. Michael lit a cigarette for Susi, then himself. "Yes, Chiara," the dark-haired reporter said. "Whatever charges they invent will be dropped, but tomorrow your father will no longer be minister. Tomorrow, we'll have a new one." Behind the haze of smoke, Michael narrowed his eyes at Angelo.

"Who?" Peter asked. "You were with him, Angelo. Who are they thinking to make the new minister? The Fascists will want one from the party, no?"

When Angelo looked at her, Chiara was waiting, the rims of her lips white. When he still said nothing, she said, "Michael said he saw you, but I told him he was wrong. My husband would never be a member of the Blackshirts. Never. But you are, aren't you? You're a Fascist." She whirled to the others, and this time there was no emotion in her voice. "Tell them. Go ahead. Tell them how my own husband and his father have conspired behind Minister d'Oro's back."

"Oh my." Susi touched the back of her turban, and her earrings made the softest tinkling sound.

"Your father has known about this for months," Angelo said. "He knows it's inevitable. The German League also made him false promises. They would have ousted him, and you know damned well that the Fascists won't put up with having a Tyrolean sympathizer as the head of the department."

Chiara nodded stiffly, her eyes fastened to his. "And you did nothing to stop it, did you? Instead, you joined the Blackshirts to your own advantage."

"I didn't want this," Angelo said. "But I have to take the position, Chiara. It's either me or someone much worse. I, at least, have the Tyrolean people's interests at heart and will do my best to make certain our developments are fair."

She scoffed and faced Michael. "I can't do this." To the rest she said, "I beg you to excuse me."

She was gone before Angelo could stop her. He stared at Michael. What could Chiara not do? He wanted to knock the smug look off the journalist's face.

Peter turned to his brother, rubbing a hand over his thinning hair. *"Du musst ihnen helfen*, Michael. For Angelo's and Chiara's sake, you get the Tyrolean peoples to accept him as the new minister. Remember, he saved me at that fair."

"Peter's right," Susi said. "The Tyroleans and the pro-German activists should not make Minister d'Oro into a martyr."

Michael squinted, took a long drag on his cigarette, and stubbed out the rest. He stood and picked up his coat and hat. Susi started to follow him but stopped at Angelo's side. Tobacco and a spicy perfume wafted from her.

"You poor boy. This is not easy. Not for anyone. You'll do the right thing. I'm sure of it."

Michael helped the countess get her cape on. *"Herr* Minister," he said, touching his hat. "A good night to you."

At Angelo's shoulder, Peter whispered, "I will talk to Michael. Susi and I will talk to him."

Angelo watched the door close behind them, relieved they were gone. As the prime candidate, he could no longer afford to have these people in his home. He would have to deal with Chiara later. Beatrice, however, was the next person he had to inform. He took in a deep breath before going downstairs to his mother-in-law.

3

GRAUN, DECEMBER 1922

The sugar biscuits for the Advent party were almost finished. Jutta put the final touches on the batch before her and checked the ones that Lisl and Sara were finishing off.

"We're almost done, aren't we?"

As if Jutta had just released a trap, Sara turned and dusted her hands.

"Where are you off to?" Jutta threw Lisl a knowing look, but before Sara could answer her, Katharina came through the back door with Annamarie and a package under her arm. She was breathless, and her swollen belly protruded beneath her heavy wool wrap.

Jutta took the parcel from Katharina and led Annamarie inside. "Did you walk all the way down like that? Your Opa's here, Katharina. He's in the *Stube* with Herr Federspiel from the bank."

"I know." Katharina sank into a kitchen chair. "It smells wonderful in here. Sugar and butter."

Sara was halfway out the door.

"You going to that construction site again?" Jutta called to her.

"No, ma'am. It's time to get Alois from school."

When she'd gone, Jutta turned to Katharina, about to explain what Sara was up to with the Italian construction workers, but at the sight of Annamarie, it would be best to keep her mouth shut. "Come here, child, and I'll give you a biscuit."

"Look at you, Katharina," Lisl said. "The way you're carrying, you're going to have a boy. You can be sure of that."

"He can't come soon enough then." Katharina took the mug of tea from her.

Jutta handed Annamarie a couple of spoons to drum with on the empty sugar pot. "So what are you doing down here? What's in the parcel?"

"Do you remember the doctor tourist from Meran? The one who was here this past summer? He ordered a jewellery box for Christmas. Florian has just finished it. I needed to get some fresh air anyway." She took another sip of tea. "Speaking of doctors, Dr Hanny is not the only one with a motorcar anymore. Did you see that Klaus Blech has one now? I saw it in his stable. What is he going to do with that thing in the winter? Certainly he won't be able to drive it around here once the snow really comes."

"It's a bit silly, I guess," Lisl said, "but it's Frederick who is worrying me. Jutta and I were just talking about how much he's withdrawn."

Jutta glanced at her, then back at Katharina. "We don't think he's ever really recovered from Fritz's death. He's distanced himself from me, which I can understand, I suppose, but from Lisl? She's his sister, for heaven's sake. Worst of all, the Blechs have really taken up with the Italians. You know why Klaus has gotten that automobile, don't you?" She waited, satisfied that she'd be the one to tell her the news. "The Blechs are now called the Foglio family. They changed their names just last week, and now there's a House Repairs Committee fixing their roof and installing new windows. And they're not the only ones." She looked at Lisl.

"You changed your name?" Katharina asked. "Tell me that's not true."

Lisl shook her head. "Georg turned the Italians down when they suggested we change it to Russo. When he found out that it meant Russian in Italian, he got very upset."

"Lisl Russo," Jutta said, making a face.

"No, thank you. I'll keep Roeschen."

"How is Georg?" Katharina asked. "I mean, after Captain Rioba took over as *podestà*…"

Lisl bent her head over the last tray of biscuits. "Quiet. Georg's been quiet."

Jutta patted Katharina's hand and gave her a *don't ask* look. "He's getting in her way, isn't he, Lisl? Always underfoot. He needs to find something to do."

"And what should that be, Jutta?" Lisl asked. "They've disbanded the fire brigade. What should he do now?" Lisl picked up a plateful of biscuits and carried them into the pantry.

In conversation these days, Jutta noted, *they* always referred to the *Walscher*, the Italians.

"Ever since Emilio Rioba's taken over as prefect," she whispered to Katharina, "Georg spends his whole day locked up in his little library. It's not good. Between him and Frederick, I don't know what to think. And some of our people keep surprising me how quickly they sell out. There's a good group of them in the valley getting subsidies in one form or the other, and the rest of us, who are holding on to our dignity, just get trouble from the authorities."

"Like what, Jutta?"

She looked disgustedly out the window. "Rioba threatened Georg with a fine if he didn't call him by his Italian title, for example."

"*Podestà*? He has to call him *podestà* or he'll get fined? That's ludicrous."

Lisl came back in and sat down with them. Jutta changed the

subject. "Your Opa's in the *Stube*, Katharina, with Anton Federspiel. They seem quite serious. Is there something wrong?"

"I'm afraid so. It's about the loan Opa had to take out last year."

"They'll figure it out," Lisl said. "Anton is fair—you know that."

"He and Hans came to new terms," Jutta added. "At least Hans has managed to make arrangements that will give him another season." She handed Annamarie another biscuit from the counter, searching the child's features for the Italian in her, something that hinted at her real father, but aside from the dark hair and brown eyes, the girl was almost the spitting image of her mother, and with Florian's dark-brown hair, it was easy to accept that she was his.

Katharina placed her mug on the table. "Jutta, when you're ready, can I get the package mailed? I still have to get to Klaus before he closes. Our sausages should be ready. Maybe Opa is ready to go too. He could walk back with us."

More news to share. Jutta slid the package from the counter, saying, "Come with me. I have something to show you."

In the hallway, they halted between the doors to Jutta's apartment and that of the new post office.

Katharina pointed at the freshly installed door. "What's this?"

"I'm no longer the postmistress. That, like everything else around here, has been taken care of by *Podestà* Rioba." She opened the door. "Good afternoon, Eric."

"Enrico. *Mi chiamo* Enrico," the postman said.

A hint of garlic wafted in the air, and the postman reminded Jutta of a rat, with a long, thin nose and beady black eyes. His long strands of greasy hair had been arranged to mask the bald patch at the top of his head, but unsuccessfully. Under the green scarf and faded brown pullover, Jutta could still see how scrawny he was. She'd never seen an uglier man, and she had certainly encountered her fair share.

"Katharina, meet Eric. Your new postman."

"When did this happen?" Katharina asked.

Jutta crossed her arms. "Yesterday. *Podestà* Rioba had my deed in one hand and the decree in the other. The builders marched right in here, blocked off the door that led from my apartment into the post office, and built the rest of this thing in a day. When they really want to be, those Italian workers can be very efficient." Loudly, she said to the rat-faced postman, "Then the *podestà* sent *him* over. Welcome to Tyrol, Eric." She touched the keys on her chain, their tone now changed due to the missing key. "Captain Rioba insisted that Eric live in one of the rooms upstairs. Lord knows for how long. Isn't that right, Eric? Are you enjoying your stay in this fine guesthouse?"

"Enrico. *Mi chiamo* Enrico."

"Apparently that's all he can say," Jutta said and shoved the package at him.

He studied the address.

"Merano." He sighed, pushing it back to her. "*Deve scrivere* Merano."

"He wants me to write something else," Katharina said. She turned to the rat man. "Do I need to change something on the address?"

"*Signora, deve scrivere* Merano." He pointed to the package.

Jutta watched over Katharina's shoulder as she took the box and pen Enrico handed to her and added an *o* to *Meran*. He told Katharina how many lire she had to pay.

"That's ridiculous," Jutta muttered. "As if he or anyone else couldn't figure out what *Meran* is."

"That one is easy," Katharina whispered.

"It might make sense." Jutta made no effort to hide her annoyance. "But how they got *Cure on Venesta* out of *Graun*, I'll never know."

"Curon Venosta," Eric said, his right hand moving in emphasis.

Jutta shot him a look she hoped would physically pierce him and walked out of the cramped space.

Behind her, Katharina spoke loudly and slowly. *"C'è tutta la posta* for Florian Steinhauser? Katharina Thaler? Or Johannes Thaler?"

Jutta gaped at Katharina's profile as Eric rummaged in his hole before handing Katharina a stack of newspapers and an envelope.

Katharina said something more in Italian, then finished with, "Thank you. *Grazie."*

He gestured a dismissal, flashed Jutta a smug look, and slammed the window of his counter shut.

"You've become awfully fluent, Katharina."

She seemed to brush the comment off as she read the top of the envelope in her hand. "Look, a letter for Florian, from Germany," she said, her tone worried. She smiled slyly and pressed her thumb to her first two fingers before moving her hand up and down. *"Germania, Signora. Germania!"* she said in a deep voice.

Jutta was not amused but gestured for the letter. There was an attorney's name and an address from Nuremberg on the back. If she were still the postmistress, she would have already known whether the letter contained good news or bad news.

She followed Katharina down the hall towards the *Stube,* but Alois burst out of the kitchen, sobbing and blubbering, with Lisl right behind him.

"What is it?" Jutta dropped down next to him and wiped his nose, searching for bruises or cuts. "What's happened to you?" She looked up at Lisl. "Where's Sara?"

Lisl threw her arms up in mock surrender. "She delivered him to the back door and left again."

Jutta would deal with Sara later. She looked Alois over to see whether he had been roughed up. That hadn't happened in a long time, but that didn't mean the bullies hadn't gotten bored. "What happened, Alois?"

"I can't go to school anymore," he shouted.

"That's nonsense. It's just the Christmas break, that's all. You'll be in school again in a few weeks."

But Alois howled, inconsolable, and then Annamarie toddled over to them, a tear forming.

Jutta looked at the other two women. "I don't know why he's so upset. He knows very well that the Christmas break is not the end of school."

Alois pushed himself off her and stamped his feet, his glasses askew. "Mistress Iris said I can't come back. She said I can't because I *non parlo italiano!*" Then, as if to emphasize his anger, he screamed again. "*Non parlo italiano!*"

"What on earth are you talking about, child?" Jutta shouted back.

Alois pulled something out of his satchel and pushed a piece of paper into her hands, sobbing. "I'm not dumb, Mother. You tell me so."

"Did that stupid cow—" Sternly, she said, "You're not dumb, Alois." With shaking hands, she unfolded the paper. After her name, everything was in Italian. There were two signatures, and from what Jutta could make of it, one was from the headmaster, the other that of the new Italian schoolmistress, Iris Bianchi.

"I don't understand a word here," she said.

Lisl looked over her shoulder. "We need a translator."

Jutta turned to her son. "What did she tell you exactly, Alois?"

"I can't go to school," he said, his voice thick. "I can't go to school anymore."

Jutta took her boy into her arms. "He's been attending that school for how many years? He's slow. Not retarded. And I am certain they are calling him that. The Italian teacher is the one who's—"

"It must be a misunderstanding," Katharina said. "Maybe if you talk to—"

"Misunderstanding, my—" Instead of letting the curse words out, Jutta threw the letter on the ground and stood to crush it with her heel. A lump hardened in her throat. How could she talk to anyone about this, much less to those school people? For instance, Mrs Blech-turned-Foglio.

"I'm not going to waste my time on idiots," she spat.

Johannes Thaler came out of the *Stube*. "What's all this noise about?"

"Let me talk to the schoolmistress," Katharina said.

Jutta was about to say she didn't need Katharina fighting her battles, but Lisl spoke first.

"That would be a good idea, Jutta. You can't take Alois with you like this. And I need to get home. Otherwise I'd stay and watch him. Let Katharina go talk to her."

"It'll be a waste of time," she snapped.

Alois sobbed and Annamarie whined.

"But if you have nothing better to do, Katharina, I guess it can't hurt."

Katharina placed her items on the small table next to the post office door and asked her grandfather to stop at the butcher shop. "Jutta needs my help. I'll come as soon as I can."

Jutta took the children's hands in hers and gave Katharina a warning look. "That teacher had better explain herself real well, or I'll march down there myself and make sure she regrets ever coming near my son."

Snowflakes drifted lightly, the breeze whipping them up in swirls, when Katharina left the inn with Lisl.

Lisl pulled her chequered shawl tighter around her neck and shoulders. "She's embarrassed, Katharina."

"About what? Alois?"

"About not being able to talk with that schoolteacher. Ever since that Italian took over the class, well, Jutta never went down there to make, you know, arrangements?"

Katharina stopped. They had reached the Roeschen home. Lisl's garden, normally lush and colourful, looked drab in the late winter, with the lack of snow.

"Nobody from the school tried to talk to her about it? Not even Mrs Blech?"

"You mean Mrs Foglio. Especially with her, no."

"That's awful. I'm surprised at Jutta."

Lisl shrugged. "You know her pride. It can get in the way. Sometimes."

Katharina smiled a little. "That's why I volunteered, I think." She glanced in the direction of the inn. "I always think of Jutta as the centre of this valley. I mean, she protects everyone here in a way, but since the Italians got here, she reminds me of a hedgehog."

Lisl was half-smiling, half-frowning. "How do you mean?"

"I mean, she curls up into herself when she feels threatened. I've never seen her so at a loss, not even with Fritz."

"All of us have a weak point, and it could be seemingly the smallest thing that breaks it." Lisl patted her on the shoulder. "Good luck then."

Katharina pondered Lisl's reference to weakness, especially relating to what Jutta had said about Georg. She could not picture their community leader sullen and withdrawn. Breaking points. What might make her break?

When she was within sight of the schoolhouse, she saw the Italian schoolmistress shaking hands with Martin Noggler's son Thomas. He laughed and said something, then walked off towards home, turning once to wave goodbye to the schoolteacher.

"Miss Bianchi?" Katharina called.

"*Sì?*"

Katharina felt nervous about trying her Italian on the teacher. In German, she said, "I'm sorry, miss, but I don't speak much Italian."

The woman smiled and beckoned Katharina into the schoolhouse. Inside her classroom, she stoked the fire, took a teapot off the hob, then moved behind her desk. She indicated to a students' bench across from her. Katharina was about to sit down, but she spotted the portrait of Benito Mussolini hanging above the teacher's head, his face slightly turned and chin raised, as if to challenge the future. Next to him, in the left hand corner on the wall, were some sentences painted in Italian. She read, *tedesco*. German. And there were negations, but she did not understand what they meant. She decided to stand.

Miss Bianchi smiled and looked at the portrait behind her. "Italy's papa," she said.

Katharina could swear she heard a touch of sarcasm.

"*Un po' di té?*" Miss Bianchi then asked, and poured two cups.

She accepted one. "*Grazie.*"

"What is your name?"

"You speak our language?"

"*Sì.* I study some before I came. But I am not so good. Excuse my mistakes, please." She stood up and moved from her desk to the bench and sat down. "Please. Seat yourself. We talk."

The schoolmistress was almost as tall as Katharina, with delicate features and long black hair that she wore in a loose bun. Her face was young, and her large brown eyes showed kindness and a hint of mischief. This did not seem like someone who would write a mean letter of expulsion.

"You a mother to child here?" Miss Bianchi asked.

"Yes. I mean, I am a mother, but she is too young to be in school yet."

"Ah. That is nice. And you expect another?" She turned an open palm towards Katharina's belly.

"Yes. I mean, *sì*."

"How can I help you?" the teacher asked.

"I am a friend of Jutta Hanny's."

"From the *albergo?*"

"The inn. Yes. She is like a mother to me. Her son—"

"Alois? You are here about Alois?" Miss Bianchi sighed and put her cup down. "Signora, what is your name?"

"I'm sorry. Katharina Steinhauser. I live in the hamlet of Arlund."

"I am Iris Bianchi. You call me Iris. *Bene?* Signora Steinhauser, about the Alois. He is sweet child, *sì?* But the *direttore*, he say Alois is—" She pointed a finger to her head and made a pitiful expression. "*Ritardo*. He learn nothing in Italian. I must to teach in Italian. He make it difficult for all here. He cry sometime when he not understand." She shrugged. "I think he old enough to work now."

"He is only eleven years old," Katharina said. "And we all know that he is slow, not mentally retarded, and he's been attending this school for years. He's always had a place here."

"Nothing. I can do nothing. The *direttore*, he here, he see class, he send me letter and tell me to sign. I sign. I can do nothing. It make me sad." Iris sighed.

"Please, Signora Steinhauser, believe me. I sad too. Alois is good boy. A good boy. But some children, they not kind to him. It make problem for me. Some children like him. They help him when the others want to fight them."

"All the more reason for him to stay on," Katharina said. "Don't you see? It's the one thing that makes sense to him. He *does* have friends here. Here, he has a place in the community."

Iris lifted her hands up and shook her head. "*Per favore*, Signora... You are too fast."

"Katharina, please. Call me Katharina."

Iris dropped her hands into her lap and smiled sadly. "You are kind. You are first person here to invite me to be friend."

"Oh dear."

"*Sì*. I know the feelings of Alois. He want to be with friends. I look for friends too." The schoolmistress gazed out the window. "Here, winter make it even more…" She turned to Katharina and flashed her a smile. "*Come si dice, desolato* in German?"

Katharina shrugged, and Iris stood and pointed out the window.

"Grey. Snow. Cold. *Così inospitale*." She stopped and smiled, the question still on her face.

"Maybe you mean dull?"

"How you say?"

"Dull."

Iris came back to the bench and sat down again. "You teach me German. I teach you *italiano. Sì? Desolato.* Dull."

Katharina repeated the words.

"*Brava.* Very good, Katharina."

She stood up. "What shall I tell Mrs Hanny?"

Iris looked thoughtful before taking Katharina's hand in hers. "I tell you not what to do, but Alois not to learn Italian because his mother not want to learn Italian, *capisce*? You understand? Children know because they feel. You must say nothing to the children. Tell Signora Hanny she need to start by doing her best too. Then, Alois, he follow."

Jutta would be as easy to melt as a glacier when it came to things Italian. Katharina could not tell Iris this. Instead, she pointed to the wall.

"What does that say there?"

Iris looked cautious. "It says, no speaking of German and no spitting on floor."

"I won't be telling Jutta that either."

The teacher smiled knowingly and patted Katharina's hand. "I talk to *direttore* again. I see if he change mind." She put a hand on Katharina's arm, and her eyes showed something mischievous. "I glad you come, not Signora Hanny."

"Why?"

"I know she not like me, and I afraid Signora Hanny come here when Alois go home. I glad it is you who come."

Katharina laughed a little. "Jutta can sometimes be difficult to deal with, this is true. But she's an important ally."

"Ally?"

"Someone you want on your side. A comrade."

"*Compagno! Sì.* With Signora Hanny, you must be on right side of fight."

"Don't worry, Iris. I will make certain you stay on the correct side."

Jutta held Florian's envelope in her hand and put it up to the steaming pot, then slid her finger beneath the fold. Luck or trouble? That was all she wanted to know. She stopped and dropped the letter to her side.

"What is wrong with me?" she muttered, and stuffed the envelope into her apron pocket.

She heard Eric-Enrico locking up the post office and stepped out of the kitchen to watch him slither up to his room. She sighed when he was out of sight, and greeted the Widow Winkler coming down the stairs.

"Disgusting man," the old woman grumbled in passing. "Put him out on the street."

"Not very Christian of you, Widow," Jutta reprimanded.

The widow peered at her, opened her mouth, closed it, then hobbled out the door without a further word. When Jutta checked on Alois, he was sleeping on the sofa, his glasses halfway up his head, his nose crusted with dried snot. What was she going to do with her child if he could not go back to school? She couldn't have Alois at the inn with the guests all the time. And obviously she couldn't count on Sara. She hung her apron on the hook on the door and went to the credenza to pull out the letter from her old school colleague. On the other side of the border, in Austria, maybe, maybe there was an alternative. She read the lines again.

There is a place here, Jutta, for children like Alois. It's not like the institutions you fear. The people are kind and care for them.

It was tempting. The money she had been saving up for her son, even when Fritz was still around, had grown, but with the inflation and exchange rate, it had lost much of its value. Besides, the institution was on the other side of the border now, and there was very restricted travel. No. There had to be a better way.

The bell rang in the hallway, and Alois stirred. Jutta glanced at him and stuffed her letter back into the drawer. Maybe the school here would take him back. When she stepped out, Katharina was brushing off the snow from her wrap.

"It's really coming down now, but I don't think it will last. The foehn wind has already started up again."

Jutta took Katharina's wrap and led her into the kitchen. "And?"

Katharina looked regretful. "I think it's a final decision, though she said she would talk to the director again."

"And you believe her? She wants Alois back in that class as much as she wants to stay here."

"Do you know where she's from?" Katharina asked. "I forgot to ask her."

"No, and I don't care."

"Jutta, if Alois learns a little Italian so that he can follow—"

"Learn Italian? Most of our children don't even know how to speak the book German correctly, not that I have a problem with that. Especially now, we have to preserve our dialect."

"Jutta, if they remain illiterate, then the Italians will be able to do what they want with us. We have to help the children prepare to deal with them, and that will only happen if they know the language."

Her ears felt hot. "If the Viennese help us like they say they will, the Italians won't be here long enough for that to happen. I can understand you feel obligated to teach Annamarie Italian. Maybe she should know who her real father is someday, but Alois, he won't be confused. He will know that he comes from, and must function, in a German society, Katharina. German."

Katharina's face had flushed. "How could you? Florian is her father. Why should Annamarie know anything about Angelo Grimani?"

"Secrets always get out," Jutta said. "Always."

Katharina looked alarmed, and Jutta drew a finger over her lips.

"Not from me." This reminded Jutta of Florian's letter. "Wait here. I've got the letter for Florian in the apartment."

She left to fetch the envelope from her apron. In the kitchen again, she found Katharina dressed and ready to go. Jutta glanced at the envelope and wondered whether Katharina suspected what Jutta's intention had been with it.

"I'm sorry if I offended you with what I've said," Jutta said. "I didn't mean to bring Angelo up."

"Mr Grimani."

Jutta nodded stiffly. "Mr Grimani, I mean."

Katharina took Florian's letter and put it into her own pocket. "I should know better. I know how strongly you feel about the Italians but—"

"Listen to me, Katharina. Those who make themselves sheep will be eaten by the wolf. You mark my words."

The girl studied her. "I am just trying to find my way here, and do my best. You'd do anything to protect those you love, I know that, but what if someone doesn't need your protection? Remember how you felt when you found out Dr Hanny knew about Fritz all along." She bit her lip and rushed to Jutta. Her embrace was brief, almost desperate.

She was out the door before Jutta had an answer.

37

4

ARLUND, DECEMBER 1922

On the way home, Katharina tried to shake off her bad
feeling. She did not want to believe that Jutta's comment
had been a threat, but there was something about her that she
could no longer understand, and ostracizing Annamarie by
revealing who her real father was might not be beyond Jutta.

Jutta was not the only one who was turning spiteful.
Resentment towards the Italians was growing all too common.
To a certain extent, Katharina could understand. The Italians
made their lives miserable, and either they had to work with
them or they would have to stand up to them and deal with the
repercussions. Yet not all the incoming Italians were bad. There
were those who came from the poorer parts of Italy and were
simply trying to make their living. Others were sent here by the
government, like the postman or the schoolteacher. Miss Bianchi
seemed to be a nice woman, and lonely. Besides, the way Jutta
and others like her were behaving was really no better than the
Italians, who held something against them just because they were
Tyrolean. Katharina bit her lip. Calling the kettle black was not
going to bring her any further with Jutta either.

Hund loped out of the stable, and Katharina petted her.

"Hi, you old thing."

She threw her a snow-encrusted stick, which the dog half-heartedly pounced on. The foehn was already coming. By tomorrow, the new snow would be gone. Inside, the house was quiet. She pulled off her wrap and boots and went to the tiled oven. It was still warm, and she rested her hands on its sides. Where was everyone?

On the table was one of Opa's newspapers, folded so as to frame a story in the middle column. She read the headline: *Captain Angelo Grimani Named New Minister of Civil Engineering.* She froze.

"It's him, isn't it?"

Opa's voice made her jump. He was standing at the top of the stairs. She stared at the headline again.

"Angelo Grimani." His voice was flat. "That was his name, wasn't it?"

There was no photograph, no sketch. Feeling nauseated, Katharina dropped onto the bench. "Where's Florian?"

"In the barn with Annamarie." Opa came down the stairs, stood at the table, and with an index finger, pushed the article towards her.

When she realised that she was reading only to find personal information about Angelo—whether he had a wife or children—she flattened her right palm over the words and stared at the back of her hand. The skin was cracked from the cold.

Opa sat down across from her. His look grazed her, and he pulled the newspaper to him. "He's a Fascist, Katharina. He's leading those projects further south where the communities have been uprooted to make room for dams and industry. In Glurns they filed petitions and objections, even hired attorneys, but all those attorneys did was convince each of the folks to sell out. Grimani won't get that far with us." He cleared his throat. "Not if you write to him."

She answered without thinking. "Why would I do that?"

Outside, Hund barked, and she heard Annamarie squealing, followed by Florian's laugh.

"He'll be involved if they go ahead with damming up the Reschen and Graun Lakes, Katharina. He'll be back here, one way or another. And he owes us. He owes you." His voice softened at the end.

"For what?" She shivered.

"For saving his life, for one."

"Then Dr Hanny should write to him. He speaks Italian."

Opa pressed his hand on top of hers. When she glanced up, his eyes bored into her. She looked past him.

"Katharina, it was Fritz *Hanny* who robbed and beat him. Grimani didn't come back up here to make trouble when the police arrested Dr Hanny's brother, but he could have. I doubt he wants to see us as much as you want to see him. Imagine he gets a letter from Dr Hanny with the same last name as the person who nearly killed him. No. You plead to his good sense of honour and making good on something he… On something he got from you."

A horrible silence followed until, from outside the window, she heard Florian and Annamarie again. With some effort, she pulled her hand out from underneath Opa's. She looked out to where her husband and her daughter were making snowballs and tossing them for Hund to catch.

"Mr Grimani got nothing from any of us but having his life saved," she said.

Opa braced himself on the table and leaned towards her, like a schoolmaster willing a schoolgirl to correct herself. She turned away and just as quickly faced him again, but he had dropped his glare.

"If you say so, girl," he muttered. "If you say so."

She swallowed a stone.

When he spoke again, he was begging. "I met with Federspiel today."

"I know." It took every effort to keep her voice steady. "What did he say?"

"He'll help us out. But it's what he didn't say…"

Katharina jerked her chin at him.

"The new Italian bank owners are demanding repayments on all loans. Federspiel can't do much more for us here. He's got little leverage left. Then there's the threat of foreclosures on a number of the farms in the valley."

"How much do we owe?"

"Enough."

Enough to worry. Enough to foreclose the farm? God forbid. She didn't care if the Thalerhof was in her name or not—this was her home. This was her land. And if things turned really bad, Florian would have too good of an excuse to pick them all up and move them to a house he owned. In Germany.

"Not as bad as Hans," Opa finally said. "If I could just help him…"

Hans too, then.

"Katharina, they build that reservoir and there'll be hundreds of families without a home. Write to him."

"To Federspiel?" She was testing him with her insolence.

Opa patiently indicated the newspaper between them.

From outside she could hear her daughter and her husband stamping their boots. "I can't."

Opa sat straight and raised his chin. "He owes us. You could reason with him."

His voice shook with anger, or with pain, or with both. She had caused that pain.

"You seemed to have been able to communicate quite well with him when he was under our roof."

He sounded like Dr Hanny on her wedding day. The stone in her throat slid past her heart, bruised it, and fell into the pit of her stomach. And Opa did not stop, no. He was picking up speed as the sounds of her family outside grew louder. She stared at her fingernails, growing white where she clutched the table's edge.

"Tell him what the valley means to us. Be rational. Tell him you want him to cooperate with us and that he has to look at the hard facts. Katharina, that ground can't hold water. Do you understand that? And if they divert that river, our farmers will have no land left. The best way to convince Grimani is if he has a staked interest in what happens to the people here. A staked interest, do you hear me?"

Annamarie burst in and tumbled towards them, her glee and innocence almost physical in the touch of her. Katharina looked at Opa just as Florian called out to them.

"I have no idea what you're talking about," she said.

Opa's look of defeat created a chasm between them, and she stood alone on the other side of it.

The dreamt of him that night: a man for whom she yearned but was never within her grasp. Angelo Grimani. In her dream, he'd been as real as she'd last remembered him, and when she awoke, the details faded so quickly they left her with the pain of a jilted lover.

She rolled over to see that Florian's side of the bed was empty, so she was startled when he spoke from the window, a silhouette against the morning light.

"You were talking in your sleep," he said.

"I was? I'm sorry."

"Never mind. I didn't understand anything." He came to her and brushed his lips on her cheek. "You were asleep before I came to bed last night. What happened yesterday? You and Opa were silent and distant."

"Nothing. It was nothing." She saw her Italian primer in his hand. "I haven't gotten very far at all with that. Were you studying it?"

He scoffed. "On the contrary, Katharina, I don't understand your need to conform."

"Conform? But, Florian, we need to know the language. I don't understand what all the fuss is about, really. It's a language."

"The fuss, Katharina, is that it's not something they're asking us to add to our repertoire. They want to forbid German completely. They're Fascists, Katharina, not damned tourists!"

"You don't need to curse," she said, but it had stung. It was Angelo's word, and she'd never heard it from Florian.

To an extent, her husband was right though. To change the focus away from herself, she told him about Alois, and when she finished, he handed her the book.

"Do you understand now what I mean?" He sighed and seemed to be mulling something over.

Anticipating bad news, she sat rigid against the headboard.

"I've been thinking," he finally said. "Maybe we should move to Germany, to Nuremberg, or even to Austria. Don't you still have relations in Innsbruck?"

"And the Thalerhof, Florian?"

"We sell it. Your grandfather told me about Federspiel's conversation with him. I think we could still get a good price. The cows, we could take them with us across the border or sell them to the Swiss. They've been coming more often for our breed."

"What will we do in a city, Florian? What should Opa do in his remaining days? This would break his heart. You know that." It would break hers.

He stood. "Rooted in tradition, I know. Hundreds of years, I know. I've heard it all before, Katharina. Unlike you, I can't see how things are changing for the better."

"It's not about that, Florian. It's about this land. My land."

He sighed loudly. Now she'd hurt him.

More gently, she said, "So we're just going to admit defeat?"

"It's a terrible way to look at it."

He went to his side of the bed and took something from his nightstand. It was the letter she'd brought him from Graun. She'd almost forgotten about it. He held it out to her. "The attorney's written regarding my mother's house."

"What's wrong?"

"Nothing. I just requested that he have an assessor look at it and tell me what the value is."

She waited.

"I could go up there, now that it's winter, and manage the things I hadn't been able to when Mother died."

"Yes, I suppose you could." He was going to leave her. She had said it aloud again, how the land was hers, not his. She'd said something in the night, called Angelo's name, and now he would leave her and the baby that was coming, and Annamarie.

"I would have to get a travel visa, but with this letter, it might not take long. I'd be back in time for Christmas, Katharina. And then we can make a decision."

She reached for his hand and held it. She didn't want to go to Germany. She didn't want him to go either, lest he realise how much better he had it without all their burdens.

"Surely we can find a way to stay here, Florian. From what the people say, the economy in Germany and Austria are not much better than here. Nor are the politics. They're just wearing brown shirts instead of black."

Florian nodded, and something in her believed he would give up on the idea, that his heart wasn't in it. Not really.

There was a knock on the door, and Opa asked whether they were planning on sleeping in. She held the primer, and as Florian finished dressing, she turned to the last page, to the vocabulary list.

Inospitale. Inhospitable. Not dull. She had to correct Iris.

She laid the book on the nightstand, feeling a tug at her heart

—that yearning she'd felt for the phantom in her dream—and a sadness settled in her, as with the loss of something dear.

∿

Florian received permission to travel across the border within days, and the night before he left, Katharina placed his hands on the baby in her belly and had him feel it moving. He fell asleep with his hands on her middle, and she did not move so as not to lose his touch.

When he was gone, the house was cavernous, what with Opa as silent as a mute. She had to do something. She decided to unload her heavy heart and try writing that letter.

The first version filled pages and pages of all that she felt about the matter: her sorrows, her regrets, and the truth about Annamarie's existence and how guilty she felt. She wrote about her growing love for Florian and her fear that he was unhappy. The next morning, she felt strangely released from the grips of her deeds and held the letter before the stove's door.

One day, she thought, the tension with the Italians would pass. It had to. One day, it would be acceptable for Annamarie to know who her real father was, wouldn't it? She stuffed the letter into her apron pocket and, after breakfast, went back upstairs, to the foot of her bed. She lifted the pine chest's lid and packed that letter away with the bloodstained shirt at the bottom. The years might eventually soften the blow.

Two weeks later and six versions of a letter she could finally send to Angelo, Katharina realised how little she knew about Annamarie's father. She had gotten up when Opa was asleep and written until her hand had cramped and the lights had gone out, and the lamp too. At first she'd tried to write in Italian, until she realised her primer was a poor substitute for making an eloquent plea. With all those drafts, she started the next morning's fire.

By the time she was satisfied with the version she could send to Angelo, she had the whole letter memorized. As a partial peace offering to Opa, she showed it to him, but she was still unconvinced by Opa's logic.

"Dr Hanny should send him our plea," she said.

But Opa said that there was surely someone at the ministry who could still read and translate German. He said nothing about the content. Instead, he told her to add the address of the geologist in Munich and gave instructions. "Georg Roeschen and Dr Hanny will know what to do when the time comes." He avoided her questioning look. "First, it has to be personal."

Next day, she bundled up Annamarie for the post office in Graun, and as they walked, fragments of the letter ran through her head. The phrases she'd kept: *Our efforts to address our concerns here in the valley have not been met with any recognition from your predecessors.* The feelings she did not commit to paper. *Are you married? Do you have children? Have you any idea what you have left behind?* Her letter had focused on reasoning with him, as Opa had suggested. *I have been asked to write to you by members of the community because they feel that the goodwill we showed you in bringing you back to health, indeed saving your life, could be the foundation of a trusted cooperation.*

Angelo had shown her compassion the last time she had seen him. The day she took the bike and chased him down, the day he played the charade at Dr Hanny's expense. She hoped he was still the same man, even if he wore a black shirt. Especially because he did so, she could want nothing further from him. Nothing at all.

Annamarie sniffed and dragged her feet. They were at the wayward cross. "Mama, tired."

"We're almost there."

"Carry."

"No, child. You must walk yourself. Your mother's got quite the weight here as it is."

She'd written about the farm, about the worries of the

farmers, who would have no land left to pass down to their future generations. Her land. Their children.

The phrases nagged her. In one paragraph, hadn't she allowed just a pinch of blackmail? Just a hint of what was at stake? Her heart jumped at the stab of panic. Maybe she should go back and strike that bit, but they were at the bottom of the road. It was too late, unless she rewrote the whole letter at Jutta's. Then she would truly have to explain herself.

She turned to her daughter. "Hurry, child, or it will just take longer."

When they reached the guesthouse, she opened the door and greeted Frau Prieth, who was just coming out, still smelling of fresh-baked bread, then slipped into the small room that served as the new post office. Before she could change her mind, Katharina handed Enrico the envelope.

"*No, Signora. In italiano. Non* Bozen. Bolzano. *Non* Südtirol. *Alto Adige.*"

"I'm sorry. You're right. You told me last time." She smiled and gestured for the pen, but the postman shook his head.

He held up a blank envelope. "*Diece centesimi.*"

"But… Ten *centesimi*? Is there gold in that envelope?"

The face of the postman remained blank. Defeated, she counted the change, and he handed her the envelope, shook out the letter, and slipped it into the new one. She filled out the information, wrote *Bolzano, Alto Adige*, and sealed the envelope.

Enrico took it with great ceremony, checked it, and shook his head. He pointed to the line that read *Ministry of Civil Engineering*, and then, as if she were slow, said, "*Italiano, Signora. In italiano. Non capisco tedesco.*"

"Now, listen here," Katharina started, and the little man pulled back as if she'd slapped him. "You better learn enough *tedesco* to tell me I have to write the whole address in *italiano*, *capisce*? You just said I needed to change Bozen to Bolzano and South Tyrol to *Alto Adige*."

"*Italiano, Signora.*" He slammed the little window shut between them and pulled down the blind.

"I need a new envelope," Katharina shouted at her reflection. There was no response except for Annamarie's whimper. "*Stupido,*" she whispered.

"What's happened?" Jutta was standing in the doorway, her keychain in her hand.

"That little swindler! He sold me an envelope because I had to change the city name, and now he says I have to write *Ministry of Civil Engineering* in Italian. How do you say that in Italian?"

Jutta scowled at where Enrico was certainly still behind the glass. "Just you wait," she scolded him. "You'll be out of a job yet. Go back to your dried-up island and eat your noodles and tomatoes again." To Katharina, she said, "Come with me. I've got an envelope for you. Don't you ever pay him another *Heller*, not for paper."

"*Heller!*" Katharina couldn't help laughing. "I could line a whole street full of the coins and only the geese and ravens would profit from them."

She waited by the sitting room window while Jutta rummaged in the drawer of her credenza. From the window, Katharina saw Iris Bianchi heading towards the church, and she turned to ask Jutta to hurry up, but she was already handing her the stationery.

"Katharina, what are you writing to the ministry for?"

"I'll tell you later." She took the envelope.

"Where are you going?" Jutta called. "What about the address?"

"I'll be back in a minute. Watch Annamarie please." She hurried to the church, hoping Iris had gone in and not farther on down the road. She found the teacher kneeling before the statue of St. Katharina, and Katharina waited until the woman had made the sign of the cross. When Iris stood up, Katharina quietly went to her and touched her on the shoulder.

"Katharina, *buongiorno*. Nice to see you."

"*Buongiorno*, Iris. I'm sorry to startle you. I did not want to interrupt while you were praying."

Iris looked up at the statue, then smiled at Katharina. "*Santa* Katharina. She help the teacher, *sì*? I pray to her for help. And here you are."

"That's right. She protects the teachers. Do you need help?"

She shook her head. "Not today. *Per precauzione*. Just in case." Iris pointed at her. "You are here to pray?"

"No. I saw you come in. It's me who needs your help."

"*Sì. Bene.* I try." She looked pleased.

Katharina retrieved the letter in the blank envelope and led Iris to a pew. "How do I write *Ministry of Civil Engineering* in Italian?"

Iris looked at her questioningly.

"They are the office in Bolzano that builds the roads, bridges, and dams." Katharina made sweeping gestures with her hands. "You know? Lots of water, held back or *whoosh*!"

"Is this government?"

"*Sì*."

"Ministry is easy. *Ministerio*." Iris gestured for a writing utensil, and Katharina fished her pencil out of her bag. "Roads? Bridges? *Genio Civile*. That must be the office."

Iris finished writing the words onto the envelope and gave it to Katharina.

"Thank you, Iris."

Iris smiled as if she was waiting to receive an explanation about the letter, but Katharina stood up, and Iris followed her out of the church without any questions. Katharina expected Iris to follow her, to return to the Blechs' home, now called the Foglios, where Iris had a room, but instead she faced north. Farther down the road, Katharina saw Dr Hanny coming in his motorcar.

"I go to Reschen," Iris said.

"Oh. Are you not feeling well?"

Iris blushed. "He practice his Italian with me. He show me his books." She shrugged. "I learn German. Tyrolean."

It made perfect sense. Dr Hanny had never married, and Iris was an attractive young woman. He had always had a taste for the exotic. Katharina had often wondered what had kept Frederick Hanny in the valley all these years when all he seemed to yearn for was a bit more of what the world had to offer. Whether the valley was ready for this liaison, however, was another issue altogether.

Katharina offered her an understanding, if not encouraging, smile. "I'll be off then."

She turned back to the inn, and when she looked up at the window of Jutta's sitting room, she saw her frowning. The sound of the motorcar made Katharina turn. She should have told Iris about the difference between the words *dull* and *inhospitable* in German. Dr Hanny was opening the car door for Iris, and Katharina smiled. It didn't matter anymore.

She turned back to Jutta, a cautious smile on her face, and waved the envelope until Jutta turned her attention to her.

Post office, Katharina mouthed.

Outside the post office door, someone whistled a lively tune that made Katharina cringe. Rioba, their new prefect. The *podestà*. He was leaning against the counter and touched his fez before moving aside to give her room. Enrico stamped something Rioba must have given him and then put his finger on the corner of her envelope. She kept her hand on it, feeling sick to her stomach.

"Just a moment," she said.

Rioba leaned over the envelope, the bronze eagle on his fez also casting a critical eye. "*Ah! Cosi si affida a vecchi amici... Brava, Signora* Steinhauser. *Ce l'ha fatta in italiano? Non era poi cosi difficile, vero? Enrico, timbra la lettera.*"

She struggled with the words, trying to understand. From underneath her hand, Rioba pushed the envelope over to Enrico, grinning as if he could not be more pleased. Enrico immediately stamped it, and the letter disappeared behind him. What if Angelo was just like these men?

"I...I'd like to have that back. *Prego.* I need to change something."

Rioba shrugged and tipped his head, the tassel of his fez brushing his brow. "*No tedesco, Signora.*"

That was a lie. The former police captain had picked up enough German from them to hold a conversation, at the very least to make it clear to them what he wanted and expected.

Her hand shaking, she paid the postage, trying to convince herself she had done all she could. If she was opening Pandora's box, then it was because she hoped Minister Angelo Grimani would prevent a flood. Not start one.

5

BOLZANO, JANUARY 1923

In the crowded gymnasium, beneath Mussolini's photographed stare, Angelo felt as if he were in a sea of Blackshirts. The party had grown exponentially under *Il Duce's* leadership.

Angelo found Gina Conti just behind him, who acknowledged him with a curt nod. Her husband stood next to her. Angelo imagined that General Conti had been made fun of as a boy for the scourge that caused the pockmarks across his face. These days, nobody laughed in the general's presence.

Signora Conti made her way towards the small group of speakers who were leaving the podium. She had her hand on her husband's arm, but Angelo was certain she was steering him and not the other way around. He remembered the Colonel's words the first time he had seen Signora Conti: she was a woman who made men.

When he turned around, his father was coming towards him.

"I need to speak to you," the Colonel said.

"What is it?"

"I've received a memo from the king about the Gleno Dam schedule."

Angelo stopped himself from rolling his eyes. "If this is about opening it by December, the answer is no. We're already strapped, especially with the two new projects up north. I cannot make further allowances on the inspections."

"Cannot or will not? You refute me every step of the way."

"Which reminds me, your permit application never came in either."

"Angelo, I expected no to be your first answer." The Colonel rubbed the back of his neck. "Kastelbell and Glurns are not to be compromised. I understand that. Still, I have to push the Gleno forward. I need the inspector's approvals to do so. Besides, it's twelve months you've got."

"Because the king wants to hold an opening ceremony before Christmas?" Angelo shook his head. "What everyone's asking for is to wring blood from a turnip. We have not seen satisfactory repairs to the mess that got started on the Gleno. Besides, you'd have to pull workers off other projects if you push it forward. That would jeopardise our state-run projects. So here's my second answer: no."

The Colonel smirked. "Come now, Angelo."

"It's my last answer."

"That's why we're talking."

As the Colonel waved Luigi Barbarasso over, Angelo noted his father's buttons straining on his suit jacket. Too much of Mama's braised veal? He had another issue, however.

"Did you pay off another one of my inspectors? He approved that plenary problem surprisingly quickly."

But Barbarasso had reached them, and the Colonel signalled he would not answer the question. The contractor and lumberman looked more similar as time went on, like two fighting bulldogs. Or, Angelo mused, the way a dog and its owner could begin resembling one another.

"Mr Barbarasso," Angelo said to his father's bulldog, "good to see you. You're looking rather robust."

"I've been taking more exercise," Barbarasso said.

Angelo followed the lumber baron's look, which seemed to devour Signora Conti in a single gulp.

"Luigi has four tons of freshly cut trees up in the northeast," the Colonel said. "He's ready to ship those to the Kastelbell Dam as soon as tomorrow. At a special price."

Angelo shook his head. "Very convenient, but he's not the supplier." He held Barbarasso's look. "You're not the supplier."

"The state will get a better price," Barbarasso said. "We can make an exchange. We provide cheaper lumber to the other projects, and you send us workers for the Gleno. It's a good deal with your budgets so strained."

Yes, Angelo thought, strained just like your coat buttons, and from whom did you steal those trees?

"Angelo, think about this," the Colonel said. "You have problems. We're offering solutions." He opened his hands. "Talk to your father-in-law. The former minister can certainly give you plenty of examples about how things get done."

"Not on my watch," Angelo snapped.

The Colonel's words had stung. Just as Pietro had suspected when taken in for questioning, the Colonel had gotten "things done" so that Angelo could be crowned Minister of Civil Engineering. Pietro, with his usual grace and dignity, had stepped aside quietly, but his acquiescence had only fuelled his team's resolve to make things difficult for Angelo. It was hardly a secret that Angelo still required Pietro's consultations on how to "get things done."

One tactic was to play the diplomat. He switched from biting to indulging. "I will look into the matter more closely. You have my word."

The Colonel smiled and shook his head. "But no promises. Now you sound like the politician. Right, Minister Grimani, keep fighting the good fight. You'll eventually see it leads nowhere but to sleepless nights." Absentmindedly, Angelo's father reached into his breast pocket and withdrew his black notebook. He just held it, as if he did not realise he had taken it out.

"There's something else, Nicolo," Barbarasso said.

"I haven't forgotten. The appeals processes, Angelo. With the new water-rights laws likely to pass by March, we can look at new projects for the future, but the objections and appeals process for the landowners is endless. We've lobbied to have those deadlines tightened. On the Reschen Lake, for example. Before they put in a caveat to buy more time."

There it was again, Angelo thought, the project that refused to leave him in peace. Sleepless nights indeed. "Perhaps I've not been communicating this clearly enough: gentlemen, we have no money left. I can hardly get the permissions from Rome to extend our budgets on the projects we do have going, much less put new ones forward or speed them up. We must begin earning something from the dams we're building before we can reinvest."

Barbarasso scratched his head and made a face. "We're working on that. As a matter of fact, Mussolini is drafting decrees for more building, and the funds will be made available. That we can assure you." He glanced around the room. "We just need some help to tide all this over until that happens. Tell us what you need, and the consortium will help you as soon as it can."

"Why is the Reschen Valley even in question again?"

The Colonel and Barbarasso exchanged a look.

"Some of our men were recently in Curon Venosta," the Colonel said. "We've done an independent surveillance on the lakes."

Angelo's blood simmered. "You were in Graun? What for?"

Barbarasso stepped forward. "Because we're still convinced there is great potential if all three lakes are raised. With the new water rights, the project will also find resonance in Rome."

The Colonel put a hand on Angelo's shoulder. "Look, when the money comes, we need a clear path. You take care of the communities and the legal aspects. Sell it to them in advance, Minister. Sell them on exactly what you're good at, the good fight." He opened to a page in his notebook and scratched something in. Angelo imagined the words *flood, money*.

"We are of the opinion that any new projects need to have a face on them, an authority figure," Barbarasso said. "What if you were to take to the road and connect with the people? Campaign for a prosperous, industrious Italy. These dams will create jobs. The farmers we relocate can work in factories. They just need to be made to recognise the advantages."

Angelo shook his head. They wanted a mouthpiece for their dirty tricks. A politician. And he was not. He was an engineer. "I'm needed here. I cannot just traipse off to the frontiers."

"You could send someone else up there," Barbarasso said. "But—"

"We believe you're the right man for the job," the Colonel said. "You already have the connections you need, people you could convince. Like in the Reschen Valley."

Angelo felt a prickling under his arms. "Such as who?"

"Captain Emilio Rioba, for example. He's been made prefect up there. You know him. The policeman who came to see you about... Well, I don't know what it was about, I suppose." His father stuffed the notebook back into his breast pocket. "He's been canvassing some of the locals up there."

A bead of sweat rolled down the inside of Angelo's arm. Maybe he should tell his father the truth about the attack on him. It was so long ago now, what difference would it make? The Colonel was waiting for an answer.

"Vaguely. I remember Captain Rioba vaguely."

"If you have your own friends up there, Angelo, connections you made during your stay there, then use them to help the cause. Before you're forced to fight against them."

"Thank you for the warning. If that's all, gentlemen, good night." Angelo winked. "I need to catch up on my sleep."

He brushed past the milling crowd to the door. Before he left, he heard his father laugh and turned to see the beguiling Gina Conti standing with the two dogs. She most certainly had the lead on them.

On his desk, a letter. Addressed to him and posted from Curon Venosta. Graun.

Someone mentioned something, and suddenly it was everywhere, crawling out of the woodwork. Months before, he'd read an article by a Victorian philosopher explaining African backwardness. While studying slaves, the philosopher had come to the conclusion that human development took place in three stages: savagery, marked by hunting and gathering; barbarism, accompanied by the beginning of settled agriculture; and civilization, which required the development of commerce. European scientists claimed that Africa was stuck in the stage of barbarism because Africans lived in a place with such good soil and climate that it provided "tropical abundance." For days thereafter, Angelo heard about the topic on every corner, in every café, and read it in other newspapers and journals, as if the world were being revolutionized by the idea. As if it would justify or change things.

On the letter from Graun, the handwriting was feminine. Arlund was where she lived. But the post office was most likely in Graun. Damn it.

Angelo loosened his necktie, sliced the envelope with his opener, and unfolded the paper. There she was at the bottom, in black ink. *Katharina Steinhauser, geb. Thaler.* Damn it. He started at the top of the letter and slammed it down.

"And now I'm supposed to be able to read German? Christ."

He could just burn it. He should destroy the letter, for two reasons. If it related to anything personal, he did not want to know what it was. If it had anything to do with his job—had she read about his nomination in the papers?—then he could choose to ignore it. The German language was dead here. He did not have to respond to anything calling on his official duties if it was not written in Italian.

He glanced at the open page. "Damn it."

On the bookshelf was the thick German-Italian dictionary. The letter was less than two pages long, but it would take him half the day to get it to make sense. He started at the top again. Certainly he could recognise a few words. Start there. *Staudamm. Plan.* It was about the dam.

Meine Tochter und unsere Kinder.

My daughter. Our children.

His head reeled while he calculated the time gone by. He had not known he was holding his breath. Those five words were surrounded by others, such as *der Grund, das Tal, die Bauern, das Leben von allen, der Staudamm.* The ground, the valley, the farmers, the lives of all, the dam. A name and address was at the bottom as well, for someone in Munich. The geological society.

It was about the dam.

He balled the letter in his fist and pressed it to his forehead. There was nothing this woman could tell him that he did not already know.

"Damn it."

Smoothing out the letter again, he rolled the end of it over the edge of his desk and ripped the bottom from the rest of it. They were worried about the dam, and there was only one way to get rid of this chapter in his life once and for all.

Minutes later he was at the desk of the main surveyor, the name of the geologist in Munich in his hand.

"Find the report from them on the Reschen Lake. And if you don't find one, get them to send it immediately."

"Yes, Minister."

"And get it to me translated in Italian. Properly."

6

ARLUND, FEBRUARY 1923

From the window in the sitting room, Katharina watched Opa hitch up his trousers and wade through the deep snow to the stable. He halted under the eaves and leaned against the wall as if a strong wind had blown him over. From the way he righted himself and from his moving mouth, she knew he was embarrassed. Then the cough gripped him, that cough that had come in on him every year since the winter of twenty. It clung to him like a creeping vine, coating the inside of his lungs and latching itself onto the smallest capillaries. The inhalants Katharina made never seemed to reach that far in, yet Opa insisted he could do all the daily chores. She did not want him to notice how she watched him, so she looked away. When he passed by the window again, he wore his feathered cap and had his hunting rifle in his hand.

She hurried to the door. "Where are you off to?"

"Snow's stopped. There'll be animals needing relief. I aim to put one out of its misery and put some meat on the table."

"Must you?"

"Cold air does my lungs good."

The sky was as clear blue as a lake, and the air was warmer

than it had been in weeks. The unseasonably warm fall had been followed by an unseasonably warm winter, until over the last two weeks the snow had fallen every day, pausing only to take a deep breath before releasing another load upon the valley.

"Then take the horse and sled," she said. "And Hund. Hund should go with you."

He gave in to her, and she was surprised, but helped him hitch Pfeffer to the sled and put a lead on Hund. "Just be home before dark, Opa." She lifted her hand, intent on stroking his wrinkled face, but stopped herself. Instead, she said, "I'd come with you. Like in the old days."

A tenderness flashed in his eyes, something she'd not seen since the Angelo Grimani resurrection in their home. He looked down at the ground, the snow almost as high as his boots. "Those were good days in bad times," he said. "You were a brave girl, Katharina. A brave girl. Still are."

A gust of wind came from the south. Watching Hund and him wade through the snow, the feather in her grandfather's cap braced against the side, she wanted nothing more than to close the distance between Opa and her. *Go with him.* She rubbed a hand over her middle. Much had changed. So much, she didn't know how to go back and make good on her mistakes.

Later, when she put Annamarie down for a nap, Katharina decided she too needed some rest. Each night, her ankles were swollen and she could never get comfortable with the baby so soon on its way. This time, sleep was instant.

It was Hund's bark that awoke her, a frantic scratching and then the banging of the front door and footsteps up the stairs. Hund. Opa. The dog must be excited about a kill they'd brought. Outside the window, it was dark already. She turned on the lamp just as Florian burst in.

"Listen." He put his hand up. "Do you hear that?"

Katharina cocked her head towards the window where he gestured. It was not a noise; it was the vibrations of the floor under her feet. Like all the children in the valley, she had learned early on that when the freeze comes too late and the snow doesn't stop, avalanches are set off like dried timber to a match. You must be able to smell it before you can hear it, feel it before it comes. And then run.

"Where is Opa?" She struggled to get up, the child in her middle weighing her down.

"Hund came back without him. I'm going out. Annamarie's crying in her crib."

"I'm coming with you."

"We haven't got time to wait."

But she was up, feeling strong. She wrapped Annamarie in the shawl and tied her to her back, then ran to the rope that led to the bell tower. She tugged and signalled the avalanche to the rest of the valley before hurrying after Florian. It was snowing again, and he was already ahead of her with the dog. The torch in his hand revealed the snow-coated tree branches, the snow-covered barn, and the tops of the fence posts of the corral. She followed him to the woods where she had seen Opa last go. Annamarie made little noises of protests. Florian turned off the torch, and the snow sizzled around them in the dark. It was easier to see this way, but she felt as if her world were upside down, like the snow globe her distant aunt in Innsbruck had once sent them.

They came to the mountain road and stopped, Annamarie and she one step behind Florian. There was no other sound save that of the snow and a light wind, until the bells began: first Hans Glockner's, then the Ritsches', then the alarm spread out to the valley. She and Florian marched on until they spotted a wall of snow piled high on the road. The scar on the mountainside was fresh, ugly, a solid, dark river in the night.

The wind howled, a deep tenor from the Karlinbach's gorge, and Katharina saw something float up into the air. A feather. She knew that feather. Opa's hat.

Sucking a long, cold breath, Katharina let out a high-pitched scream until she was out of air. She inhaled again, and this time one stab after another tore through her middle. She gasped and sobbed. It was Florian's arms she fell into and Annamarie's shriek she heard before the barrier between her womb and the cold world broke.

Under the thick covers, Katharina slid deeper into the soft darkness, into safety. She would eventually have to face what awaited her: Opa's funeral arrangements. The people downstairs conducting the visitation. Her baby—Florian's son. Florian. Annamarie. The house was filled with people, yet the emptiness in her was absolute.

She shut her eyes tight but heard the voices outside the door and then the baby crying like an abandoned kitten.

"She won't take him."

"Give her time." It was Hannelore.

"But she won't even look at him." Florian again.

"She's grieving." That was Dr Hanny. "Give him to me."

When a soft knock came at the door, it took every bit of her energy to sit back up. Dr Hanny stepped in, holding the bundled infant.

"I'm bringing your son to you."

She saw Annamarie peek around from behind Hannelore's legs, caught sight of Florian's concerned face, and was relieved when Dr Hanny gently closed the door on them.

"Hannelore will come in just a moment. I thought you should have the baby. And we could talk about your grandfather, the avalanche."

He handed her son to her, and Katharina pulled away the edges of the blanket to look at the baby's face. His eyes were swollen, like Annamarie's had been when she was born, and his skull a little cone shaped. As Dr Hanny took a chair from the corner of the room, Katharina put the baby under the bedcovers and helped him to take her breast.

She looked at Dr Hanny. "And how long until I feel something for *this* one?"

"You love both of your children. You are in a state of shock. Your grandfather—"

"At the same time as *he*"—she lifted her arm where her son lay —"decided to come into the world." She felt his tiny hand against her breast. "Do you think my grandfather's spirit entered him?"

"It's a nice idea, but strictly from a scientific point of view…"

"You, Doctor, have always been the one to say that the best state of health must come from here"—she bowed her head— "and the spirit."

"Yes."

"My head and my spirit are sick."

"Grief."

She shook her head. "Disappointment. Regret."

"I'll fetch Hannelore. The midwife will be more familiar with your malady."

A tear rolled down her cheek. "Is grief, is regret, simply a malady?" When Dr Hanny did not answer, she said, "I should name our son after Opa. But Florian and I had planned to name him after my father."

"Josef Johannes then."

Katharina tried to look pleased.

"It's a good name. A strong name. There's nothing wrong with it."

"What's wrong with me then?" she asked.

"What do you need?" He was reaching for his medical bag.

"Forgiveness."

"Maybe you need a priest then, not a doctor." His smile, a failed attempt. "What do you want to be forgiven for? By whom?"

She had revealed too much already. She moved the baby to her other breast.

His voice was extra gentle when he said, "You forget that I was there."

She locked eyes with him.

"The day Johannes sent him away," Dr Hanny said. "That day you ran after him."

So it was true. Dr Hanny knew Annamarie was Angelo's daughter. And Opa had too then. If she tried to deny she did not know what Dr Hanny was talking about now, it would make things worse. It would make her lie unbearably gross. She said nothing.

"Your daughter is a strong, healthy child, a blessing. Your husband is a good, honest man. And Annamarie knows him as her father. There is no shame in that." Dr Hanny patted the blanket near her leg. "You could start all over, you know? It's a blessing amongst the living to be able to do that."

He left her then, and Katharina felt as if she would implode from sadness. Her thoughts swirled. Angelo had never acknowledged her letter, and she had not known how much she had hoped to hear from him until this very moment. She had mentioned a daughter. Had the man not enough sense to suspect he had left her pregnant? If he were honourable in any way, he would have answered her. One way or another. Opa, God bless his soul, had stopped himself from prying the truth from her again. She had been dishonest with him under his own roof. Now it was too late to apologise.

The knock at the door startled her, and the baby twitched in his sleep. Florian came in, and even from that distance, she could smell the wood shavings on him. He'd been sawing and hammering the day before. Her husband, the "stranger," had built Opa's last resting place. She needed this man now. She needed him to be close to her, to belong to them.

With their son hugged up against her, she said, "Let's name him after your father. Let's name him Bernd."

They were all waiting for her in the sitting room, where Opa had been lain out on the table beneath the crucifix. Already, from the top of the stairs, Katharina could see her grandfather was completely altered. The rose-coloured cheeks were chalky and thick with some sort of paste that had been used to cover up the bruises and wounds. One of the women had washed and made him up—Hannelore, maybe? Jutta?—and dressed him in his one good suit. And his shoes. The new boots Florian and she had bought him last Christmas. The ones he'd refused to wear, saying he'd save them for a day when he'd really need them. Would be a shame to bury those now, but she couldn't just march over there and pull them off, could she? Scold her Opa and ask him, teasingly, what he was thinking?

Katharina descended into the murmuring of women's voices: *Our Father, who art in heaven...* Prayers for the dead. Into the hushed clinking of glasses. She turned her head to look at the second table, the one they'd brought in from outside.

There were cups of wine and schnapps glasses scattered across the surface, with two empty bottles and two that were half-full. There were people everywhere, and only then did she scan the faces, some politely, sympathetically smiling and looking away, others nodding at her as if to give her strength or tell her they understood.

Everyone was here. Dr Hanny, Hannelore, the Prieths, Hans Glockner, and the Nogglers. Even the Planggers had come all the way over, and Karl Spinner.

She heard someone mutter, "...farm's going to outsiders," and searched the men standing around the oven, but she'd not recognised the voice, and there was a whole group of them oblivious to her. Her chest constricted.

Outside the windows, she could see the visitors who had spilled out into the *Hof* like an invasion of shadows. She pressed

Bernd closer to her as she submerged herself into the lot of them. Jutta, Frau Prieth, Frau Plangger, and Patricia Ritsch were sitting on the stools they'd set up in order to pray around Opa. They stood when she approached, and Katharina looked upon the man who'd been her last anchor in this community.

She felt someone touch her shoulder, and Father Wilhelm offered his hand. Katharina took it and squeezed, and then the procession of condolences started. Jutta hugged her before taking Bernd, thankfully without much comment, so that Katharina could accept the stream of handshakes. Her community. Their valley. Some did not look her in the eye, but offered their hands anyway. She'd not paid enough attention to know who would help her in the future and who would turn against her. And Opa could not help her differentiate between the two now.

Patricia Ritsch stepped up, her own infant, Andreas, in her arms. Of course Toni would name his first son after the freedom fighter.

"They will be famous friends, Katharina, our two boys." Patricia smiled, and then she must have felt awkward, because she swallowed and looked down, her cheeks flushed.

"They will, Patricia," Katharina offered. She placed a hand on the woman's upper arm and squeezed gently. "Thank you."

Anton Federspiel stepped up, Frau Prieth, the baker, just behind him. Katharina held her breath. Certainly Anton had enough decency not to mention the finances now. She shook his hand, and Anton whispered something about how everything would be all right. Her thoughts whirled with the possible interpretations, but she could not make heads or tails of it. As she greeted Frau Prieth, the door opened and Iris came in, her face drawn and her eyes skittering until they landed on Katharina. Her relief was visible, her look of regret immediate. Katharina's heart swelled with a tenderness and a dread she did not know she had space for now.

Behind Iris, Toni Ritsch stepped in with his father, so near to Iris that she had to step aside to let them through. The men held a schnapps glass each, Toni's nose red from obviously too many already. As he passed Iris, Toni eyed her up and down, scowling, swaying a little. As if oblivious to his son's bullying, Kaspar Ritsch came directly to Katharina and patted her shoulder, telling her Opa would get a hunter's funeral. He'd arranged it.

Katharina thanked him, and he left her to pray at Opa's side.

When she looked for Toni, he was hovering near the table with some of the other men, his glass filled with schnapps. He was staring at Iris, and even she could hear him say, "The old man would turn over if he knew the *Walscher* was here."

"Where's his rifle, Kaspar?" Katharina whispered at the old man's shoulder. "Where's Opa's weapon?"

"We recovered it before the *carabinieri* came," he whispered back, turning only slightly to her.

"I want it, Kaspar. I want it for protection."

His was a mix of pity and caution. "We have to turn it in, Katharina. You don't want to risk having contraband found."

"Talk to Florian. Invent a story that we didn't recover it."

"But when the snow melts... Listen, the *carabinieri* were already asking Dr Hanny about it."

"Please. Please talk to Florian."

Kaspar nodded, but she knew he was not taking her seriously. The thought that Toni, or even Kaspar himself, might squirrel away the rifle for themselves, for their stupid uprising, crossed her mind.

After the Planggers greeted her, Katharina moved from the table to Iris.

"I should not have come," Iris whispered in greeting, and Katharina took her hand and squeezed it.

"I am glad you did, but maybe you're right. Please know, I do appreciate it."

She was relieved when Dr Hanny came to them and gently led

Iris to the corner with Father Wilhelm. Iris had two more friends amongst them who would stand up for her if need be.

Katharina had to find Toni, but he was no longer in the house. He'd not come to her. He'd not given her his hand. Instead, she went to Jutta, who stood with Hans near the oven, and took the baby from her.

"I'll slaughter one of my sheep today, if you want," Hans said to Katharina. "For the soup."

"That's fine, Hans. I'll have Florian pay you straight away."

Hans looked embarrassed. "I'll make a good price."

"Don't worry, Hans." She excused herself and went outside, where she found Florian standing with Martin Noggler and Kaspar Ritsch. Still no sign of Toni.

"Husband, Hans needs some money for the mutton. For the funeral soup. Did Kaspar talk to you about the rifle?"

"We can't keep the rifle, Katharina."

Holding back her exasperation, she returned to the other issue. "Where's Toni? I thought he was with you."

Kaspar pointed to the corner of the house, where Toni, his back turned to her, was leaving with Patricia. "They're on their way home. Do you want me to get him?"

"What's wrong, Katharina?" Florian asked

"Did he give you his hand?" she whispered to him.

Florian shrugged. "There's a lot happening at the moment. I don't know. Why?"

Of course, this was all new to him. He did not understand how serious a gesture this was. She watched Toni and Patricia disappear around the house. Hot tears came to her eyes.

It was not from the Italians she felt an overwhelming need to protect herself.

∼

On the day of the funeral, Katharina sat perched on her side of the bed, her back to her husband and looking at the sleeping infant in his cradle. The frost on the windowpanes was hardened into snowflake shapes, and the ice beneath the eaves dangled like clear-cut stalactites. She could hear the cows rustling in the barn, their tapping hooves like the impatient drumming of someone's fingernails on a tabletop.

It had never been spoken aloud. It had hung in the air between them, and now here it was: Florian Steinhauser, an outsider, a city man, would be the new owner of the Thalerhof. The farm had only half the cattle it once had in its best days, and now their last horse was also gone. There were two children to tend to, and the debts that had accumulated were left unpaid.

Florian stirred next to her, then sat up, alert. "Why didn't you wake me?"

"We're all tired."

"I'll go to the barn," he said, already pulling on his shirt. "The children?"

"Still asleep."

It was a miracle really. As if the energy in the whole house was drained. Even Bernd fell into a deep sleep each time she nursed him. She sat where she was, shivering, unable to summon the energy to get up. She heard Florian pause behind her.

"Are you all right?" he asked.

Katharina turned stiffly to him. "The farm's yours now. You will have to see Anton Federspiel at the bank, and the registrar to fill out the paperwork. And Bernd's birth certificate."

Florian paused in buttoning his vest. "It's still the Thalerhof."

"The deed will have your name on it."

"It's just a piece of paper," Florian said. "The sign above the door will still be your name."

Nothing really belonged to him except on paper. Their daughter had his name, but not his blood. The farm would legally be his, but the name and its reputation, never. His clothes had belonged to other people, and even she had lent herself to him in the beginning. Bernd was his only legacy. At least, so far. And Annamarie? With a son now, Florian truly had no obligations to Katharina's daughter anymore. He certainly had no obligations to the Thaler family. What he did still have was his mother's house in Nuremberg.

"Well, you could just sell everything here and drag us to Germany now."

Florian froze in his dressing.

"I'm sorry," she said. "I don't know why I said that."

He smoothed down his vest and quietly left the room, the door clicking softly behind him.

It would be his decision in the end, though after he had returned from Nuremberg, she had overheard him telling Opa that the economic situation was—as she had guessed—not much better than here. As for his mother's house, he'd not yet decided whether to sell it.

By the time she had Annamarie dressed for the funeral, the death bells were already tolling, the largest to the smallest ringing in succession. She met Florian coming out of the barn, and he threw icy water on his face and upper arms before rolling down his sleeves and slipping into his overcoat and joining her, in silence, on the road to St. Anna's hill.

Later, as they neared the church, she could see the cemetery wall and the gathering in front of the chapel. At their arrival, the whispered condolences and light handshakes were repeated as in the wake, and Katharina swam through the villagers as if grasping at debris, looking for someone to pull her out of the flood of grief.

Father Wilhelm came to them, but Katharina found it difficult to concentrate. It irritated her that the priest led Florian to the altar next to Opa's coffin and whispered about whatever needed whispering about. It was Jutta's touch that turned her attention away from it all. She handed her Bernd.

"He's beautiful, Katharina," she said. "I wanted to tell you that at the visitation, but thought I'd wait."

"Florian's pride and joy."

Jutta grasped her hand but said nothing.

Father Wilhelm started the service, and Florian took his place next to her, but Katharina could not remove her eyes from Opa's coffin. She went through the motions, and at one point Annamarie whimpered and Katharina realised she was squeezing her hand too hard. She bent and kissed the girl's head, drawing her closer to her skirts.

In the cemetery, the hunters had hung up an enormous wreath with a green ribbon, and Karl Spinner and Kaspar Ritsch were dressed in their hunting costumes. They led the singing—"Aufwiedersehen"—and loneliness overcame Katharina as she wept for the first time.

All her loved ones lay under the ground. Her last living relative on her father's side was gone. Johannes Thaler had dreamt of leaving his legacy to his sons. Had even considered her worthy enough to own the land, to take over the Thalerhof. And she had merely proven herself unworthy. And the valley folk would not make it any easier for Florian.

She looked at her husband and, as with many times before, wondered at the practical stranger who had taken on the responsibilities of becoming a husband, a farmer, a father to a bastard child.

Start all over, Dr Hanny had said. It was he who had probably imparted the same wisdom on Florian. Katharina would never be able to forgive Dr Hanny if Florian packed them up and made her leave the Thalerhof for Germany.

Four days after the funeral, Florian asked Katharina to go to the registrar's with him to handle the death certificate, the transfer of the Thalerhof's deed, and Bernd's birth certificate. She bundled up the children, and they walked to the office that once used to be Georg's. In a few minutes, she managed to communicate to the official what they were there for. They started with the birth certificate.

"*Nome?*"

"Bernd. Bernd Steinhauser."

Without raising his head, the registrar rolled his eyes. "Bernd?"

"*Sì.*" Katharina gestured for him to give her the pen so she could write it down. When she turned the scrap of paper to him, he sighed as if the weight of the world were on his shoulders, but wrote into the form.

"*Il suo nome e Benito.*"

"What did he say?" Florian asked.

She examined the birth certificate the registrar presented her. She could not believe what she was reading. "He wrote that his name is Benito Casa de Pietra."

The registrar waved his pen at them, then indicated the portrait of Benito Mussolini. *Il Duce*, as his followers called him, the Leader.

"*Sì, sì.*" The registrar nodded enthusiastically. "*Casa de Pietra.* Steinhauser." He said their German name as if he were chewing on glass.

Florian grabbed the document, then looked at the registrar. "You understand enough German to be able to translate our name into Italian? In that case, you will understand this: my son's name is not Benito. It is not Casa de Pietra. His name is Bernd Steinhauser, and you will now change it to reflect that." Florian pushed the document back at the glaring registrar.

"Signor Steinhauser, it would be wise of you to consider changing your name to an Italian version," the registrar said. His accent was heavy, and the high German sounded wholly out of place.

"You would like the deed to your farm to reflect you as the owner—then you should know that the generous Italian government is prepared to help fund any repairs you may need to create a sturdier, more comfortable home for you and your lovely children." He looked as if he felt badly about it. "But there are certain criteria—"

"I am a carpenter," Florian said stonily.

The registrar wobbled his head. "You are looking for a job?"

"No. I don't need your cursed funds. I can take care of my family myself."

"As you wish. Here are the forms. The deed?"

Katharina fished the deed and Opa's death certificate out of her bag and handed them to the registrar, her heart thundering.

Just a glance at the document first before the registrar said, "You must have both translated into Italian. All formal documents must be filled out in Italian, and if you wish to have the deed transferred into your husband's name, you will have to present us with an Italian version."

"But you speak German," Florian said, his voice a pitch higher than normal.

"I can do it for you. For a fee." A flash of teeth.

Katharina pulled on Florian's coat sleeve. "We're done here for now, husband. Thank you for your offer, Signor. We will see to it ourselves."

"As you wish," the registrar said, and turned back to his books. Before they were out the door, he called them back. "Signor Steinhauser, I am just reminded. Signor Giovanni Thaler, he was a hunter, no?"

Katharina stared at Florian. This was about the rifle.

"Johannes Thaler," Florian corrected him. "Yes, he was a hunter."

"The rifle?"

"It was lost in the snow. You'll have to wait until spring, after the melt."

Katharina felt the heat rising to her cheeks, and at that moment she loved her husband fiercely.

The registrar made a face. "Ah, *sì*. You believe me to be a fool. I understand."

Florian shrugged. "Believe what you wish. I'm telling you, the rifle is lost beneath all that snow. I will bring it to you in the spring."

The registrar raised his pen, licked the tip, and flipped at a little booklet to his right. "So in April? You will bring it in April?" At the book he muttered in Italian, which Katharina understood well enough by now, "Or in this godforsaken place, it might be June."

"April," Florian said.

"It must be April," the registrar said menacingly, "or you stay in jail until we find it. *Capisce?* It is the law." Again the feigned apologetic look.

Florian's jawline flexed. "Yes."

"Signor Steinhauser? I remember now. You are not a citizen here, is that correct?"

Neither Florian nor Katharina answered.

The registrar looked at her, then at Florian. "You don't like our laws, you can always go back to Germany."

Katharina's heart dropped, and she tugged on Florian's coat again until he finally went out the door with her.

"Leave the translation issue to me," she said outside. "Why don't you go to the inn? Jutta and Hans are waiting for us. I'll go find Iris."

"Iris? The Italian teacher?"

"The schoolmistress and I know one another, and she's helped me before. Florian, ignore that man. He's only trying to provoke you."

He looked uncertain, but she bent to her daughter to make sure she was well bundled. She froze when she heard whistling and knew who it was before he stopped in front of them: the prefect, Captain Rioba.

"*Buongiorno, Signora* Steinhauser. *Con tutta la famiglia questa volta?*"

Katharina could feel Florian simmering next to her, but she felt a little thrill deep below the terror. She was beginning to understand what these people were saying. The prefect had asked if she were here with the whole family this time.

"I hear from your grandfather's death," the prefect continued in German. "I am sorry. To both of you."

Katharina gave him a stiff nod, remembering how he'd made no effort to clarify himself to her at the post office the last time she'd seen him.

"Did bank contact you about money owed?" Rioba asked. "I have tip for you, a clue."

Florian stepped forward, his cheeks flushed. "We will take care of those debts as they were arranged between Johannes Thaler and the bank."

"*Sì, sì,* I certain you will. But perhaps you know that you have big opportunity to buy off—no, *scuzi,* who can buy land these days? I mean sell off your land. Italian government put together offers for all properties where dam may be, *capisce?*"

Florian shook his head. "There have been no formal plans for the dam. And surely none that would affect Arlund."

Rioba looked concerned. "No? Ah, they are coming. They are coming."

He winked at Katharina, and her heart galloped.

What if her letter had only provoked Angelo Grimani? He was a Fascist now. What had she done?

"No need to alarm," the *podestà* continued. "You transfer deed into your name. They make offer when it is so far. Then you talk with them, eh? How do you say? We sing all from same songbook in the end." He bent down and chucked Annamarie under the chin and looked up at Katharina. "*Bella, come la mamma. E questo è l'ultimo!* And here you have a new baby. A lad or lass?" he asked, using the Tyrolean slang for boy or girl.

"A boy," Katharina said.

"*Come si chiama?*" Rioba asked, looking at Florian. "What his name?"

"Bernd," Florian said.

Rioba lit up. "Benito! *Splendido!* Named after *Il Duce*, he will go far."

7

GRAUN, APRIL 1923

A nother funeral, and just months after Johannes Thaler's. From her kitchen window, Jutta dabbed her eyes with the corner of her apron as first the pallbearers then the mourners spilled out of St. Katharina and into the drizzling rain. At the sight of the tiny coffin, her heart felt heavy.

Melanie, the Planggers' youngest. She'd just turned six when the melt spilled over the riverbanks, taking her with it. It almost sucked in the other three youngsters who had been playing with her at the Planggers' tree. Jutta ought to be with Maria Plangger now instead of cooking for the wake, but Sara had run off in the night, most likely with the Italian builder, that he-man who had lurked around the back fence of the Post Inn.

When Katharina—the baby in her arms—and Lisl appeared in the procession, Jutta rapped on the windowpane until they realised she was trying to get their attention. The women hurried through the back gate, and when they were in the kitchen, Jutta explained the emergency.

Katharina placed Bernd in an empty apple crate, while Alois tugged Annamarie to a place where they could play.

"We were wondering why you weren't in church," Katharina said. "What can we do?"

"I haven't got the strudel ready yet," Jutta said. "The apples are over there. There's all this food the farmers brought, but I've got the soup finished. Alois is out there pushing the tables to make one long one..." She was about to say, *like we had for your Opa*. "... per usual. One long table. And the wine jugs, of course, and the schnapps. There's not a soul here who can be measured as being wealthier or poorer. Everyone gets soup today."

Lisl looked over Jutta's shoulder at the *Knödel* dough. "I'll roll and boil those. You get to the potatoes."

"That little chit," Jutta muttered. "Sara knew the funeral was today."

"Scandalous, really," Lisl agreed. "And to leave you all alone with Alois. Maybe she'll come back."

"She had better not," Jutta said. "If I ever get ahold of her, she'll be sorry about a lot more than leaving me high and dry."

She turned to the potatoes just as the Widow Winkler barged through the door. "I will not be buried with that husband of mine!"

Every time. With every funeral.

"Yes, Frau Winkler," Jutta said. "We know. That's why you bought into the plot at St. Anna's with the Blechs. I mean, the Foglios."

"What?" the old widow yelled. "Foglios?"

Katharina made a noise like held-back laughter. "She means Klaus Blech. He sold you his plot on St. Anna's hill."

The widow was not pacified. "I won't be buried with him. Herr Winkler's in hell, and I won't be buried with him, and not with Klaus Blech either, that *Walscher* lover. Not with anybody..."

Jutta nodded. "Not with anybody going to hell. We understand."

Katharina dropped the apple she was peeling, shaking her head. Lisl was also smirking. When she realised nobody was paying attention to her anymore, the widow left with one last indignant huff.

"Jutta Hanny." Katharina laughed when the door closed behind the old woman.

"What? Klaus signed the pact with the devil when he changed his name." She remembered the Steinhausers' predicament. "Katharina, have you heard anything about the deed to the *Hof*?"

"Nothing yet. Every time we ask, they say to check next week."

Lisl clicked her tongue. "Even in the worst of times, our bureaucrats were more efficient."

"Well, it took a while with mine," Jutta reminded them. "And then I got a new post office to boot."

"It doesn't feel right." Katharina frowned. "And I can't shake that conversation with the prefect."

"Captain Rioba?" Jutta looked up. "What did he say?"

A shadow passed over Katharina's face. She shrugged. "Something about buying and selling, and it made Florian think that things are really getting serious about raising the lakes. Otherwise, why would the Italians be interested in purchasing land?"

Lisl dipped the slotted spoon into the pot of dumplings. "Or pushing them off. But, Jutta, they would be talking to you first, and the church, don't you think? Those are the two most important properties for them."

Jutta shook her head. "I wanted to believe that the Italians would honour our appeals. Forget our little frontier. But that's too much to ask, isn't it?"

Lisl put her spoon down and leaned on the counter. "It is, Jutta. Every time the water runs over the Etsch, we look to the lakes. Every time a new machine or new technology appears in the valley, we look to the lakes. Every time the lights go out, we all look to the lakes. Georg says they will build a reservoir here whether we want it or not. There's nothing we can do."

"Nothing?" Jutta remembered the letter then, the one she'd never asked about again—the one Katharina had sent to the Ministry of Civil Engineering some months ago. She scolded herself for forgetting, but she would not address it in front of Lisl.

"Either way," Katharina was saying, "until we get the deed, the farm is in what Florian calls no-man's-land."

Over her shoulder, Jutta scoffed. "That's what they're calling us in general. People without a country."

She dumped the potato skins into a bowl with the other vegetable and fruit peels just as Alois came in with an empty tray. "Alois, take these to the compost pile and dump it clean." She turned to the women. "Speaking of threats to our land, you must keep this to yourselves, but Hans has real troubles."

Katharina sighed. "I know he was looking to borrow more money, but—"

"Federspiel denied his application and warned him of foreclosure. He told him the bank would like to continue working with him, was very sympathetic, but said the Italian bank owners are getting very pushy." She sighed. "What I wouldn't do to help him out."

Lisl hopped behind the counter like a small child at Christmas. "Jutta? Are you going to marry him?"

"Heaven's no, woman." She axed a potato. "I just want to help a friend." Behind her back, she could feel their questioning gazes, but she looked out the window. He still had not asked her. Fritz had been dead two years, and Hans still had not asked her. What was stopping him now was the threat to his farm. What was stopping him was his foolish shame.

The blossoms on the apple tree were not quite yet open, and she could see the tops of people's heads over the cemetery wall. At the compost pile, Alois was playing with the peelings, dropping them from the bowl by the finger-full.

"What is that child doing now?" She shouted through the

window, "Alois, hurry up now. Stop playing with that garbage. Girls, they'll all be here soon."

Lisl was just draining the *Knödel*, and Katharina brought her the sliced apples for filling the strudel and left for the *Stube*. It was not for several minutes that Jutta realised Alois had still not come back. When she looked outside, she saw Rioba leaning against her gate, talking—yes, talking—with her son.

She went out the back door. "Alois, time to get inside. Annamarie's waiting for you."

The prefect waved at her nonchalantly, and Alois half skipped, half ran on his thick legs back to the house. She gave her son a cursory glance and then shoved him inside. "What did he want with you?"

"To practice his German." Alois sniffed.

Rioba always put on a show about how important it was for everyone to understand *him*. Why would he be practising German with her "mentally retarded" son?

From the window, she saw the mourners filing out of the cemetery. "They're coming," she announced. For another moment she watched the prefect leaning against the fence. He was holding something, but she could not make out what it was.

When Katharina came in from the *Stube*, she told them that Henri had arrived and she had delegated the bar to him.

Jutta nodded, grateful. Lisl's sons were doing fairly well for themselves. Paul was reading the law and would soon be an attorney. David was interested in agriculture. Only Henri, the middle one, seemed to have not yet found a purpose.

"Lisl," she said on impulse, "if Henri wants it, I have a job for him, right here at this inn. With Sara gone, he can have it now. The people like him, he's good at it, and it suits him."

Lisl smiled. "Why, Jutta. That's very generous."

"It's settled then. I'll talk to him about it later today. Will you serve the soup?"

As soon as she put the pastry into the oven, she could hear the people coming into the front hall and sent the women out to meet them while she quickly cleaned up the kitchen. The sound of raised voices in the yard drew her to the back door once more.

Near the oak tree between her inn and the church, Hans and Florian were facing off with two *carabinieri*, Hans pounding a fist into his other hand, and Florian waving an arm at the mountains behind him. Rioba also looked serious as he talked with Father Wilhelm.

"Jesus and Mary. Now what?" Jutta stripped off her apron and was swiftly outdoors and at their side. She saw that one *carabinieri* was holding an Italian flag.

"What's going on here?" she demanded.

Pointing a finger at Captain Rioba, Hans said, "He wanted Father Wilhelm to consecrate their flag, but Father Wilhelm refuses. And this one"—Hans scowled at the second policeman— "shoved Father Wilhelm."

"You shoved back," Rioba said, as if they were all kindergartners. "Not good with police. You not shove police."

Father Wilhelm turned on Rioba, his eyes glowering. Jutta had never seen their priest this angry.

"This flag belongs to a country whose government is run by tyrants," he shouted. "And your king was excommunicated. I too have my superiors to answer to."

Captain Rioba slowly shook his head, then waved a dismissing hand at the other two *carabinieri*. They threw Florian and Hans menacing looks but obediently left the yard.

Rioba lifted his fez and smoothed his tight black-and-grey curls before fitting it back onto his head. "I not arrest you, *padre*, because you no bless *bandiera*," he said, lifting a finger. "Or you shoving my men." He had a warning gleam in his eye, and he leaned forward as if to whisper to Father Wilhelm, but he was loud enough for all to hear. "When I find what I look for, I will arrest you for the *scuola*."

Father Wilhelm took a step back. "What school?"

Jutta clutched her throat. How did Rioba find out about the school?

The prefect cocked his head and gave the priest a patronizing smile. "*Clandestino.* The under-the-ground school. You, *padre*, are headmaster. I see in your eyes, you all know I right. You are a priest—you cannot lie."

"Come with me," Hans said. "We'll take care of this later."

"But—" Jutta started.

"Come with me," Hans repeated. "All of you. There's a wake to attend."

Florian and Father Wilhelm obeyed first and turned towards the inn. Jutta put her hand on Hans's arm and let him lead her away, but before they could take three steps, Captain Rioba whistled. As if they were dogs to call back. But they all turned in their tracks, like obedient animals. She could not look Rioba in the face.

Behind Jutta, Florian said, "What do you want?"

"Forget your attack on Italian police." Rioba's voice was grave. "You pay something to policemen, make hurt pride go away, we forget incident. But *padre* Wilhelm more serious. We find proof for *scuola*, he go away a long time. And everyone with him." He sniffed, turned his back on them, and strode off, whistling a slow and mournful tune.

Hans's arm flexed beneath Jutta's hand. They all returned to the guesthouse wordlessly until they reached the back door.

"We have to find Frederick," Florian said. "We have to get the warning out about the school and see if he can negotiate with Rioba."

The hall and the *Stube* were crowded with people for the funeral. They pushed their way through, Jutta half greeting and half checking on the guests. She stopped to offer her condolences to the Planggers and left Father Wilhelm with them. When she and the others found Frederick, he was standing at the back of the *Stube* with that Italian schoolmistress and Katharina.

83

Katharina, too, was always going to that teacher. What did those two possibly have in common?

"Frederick, we need you," Jutta said and cast that Iris woman a look to let her know she was not welcome.

"Father Wilhelm is in trouble," Florian said at Jutta's elbow.

"They wanted him to consecrate an Italian flag, and he wouldn't," Jutta explained.

"It's not about the flag," Hans said. "The prefect—" He stopped, his eyes on the schoolmistress.

Iris slipped sideways between them with a quiet "*Scuzi.*"

"Frederick," Jutta whispered when Iris was gone, "they found out about our school."

"How?"

"Alois must have said something," she told them. "I saw him talking to Captain Rioba out in the yard."

Their eyes grazed her. Those brief looks of accusations were quickly veiled over with pity, then understanding. It gnawed at her.

Hans put a hand on her shoulder, his beard trembling as his jaw worked. He didn't have to remind her. He had once suggested that sending Alois to Father Wilhelm could be too dangerous, but she had protested, even told him that he was being unkind. In truth, she had been desperate to send Alois to the lessons. Now their priest was in danger.

Frederick put his wineglass on the table behind him. "Where's Father Wilhelm?"

Jutta pointed to where she had left him with the Planggers.

"Hans, Florian, come with me." Frederick brushed by Jutta and stopped in front of the schoolmistress. He bent over her hand, clicked his heels together and looked apologetic. He went to Father Wilhelm.

Jutta waited until they were gone before turning to Katharina. "Frederick is, in all seriousness, courting that woman, isn't he?"

"You mean Iris Bianchi?"

The schoolteacher was standing alone and out of place. She was a reed, with dark features, thin lips, and a head full of thick hair swept into a bun save for the stray strands that curled above her collarbone. She wore city clothing, the hem of her navy-blue dress outrageously high above the ankles, and she also wore stockings with a pair of patent leather shoes and heels. In the hinterlands!

"With skinny ankles like hers, that woman won't last long. It's her fault, you know. We wouldn't have this problem if she weren't here."

"Iris could help. She does have a good heart."

Jutta snorted. "So Frederick *is* courting her? I thought it was just a passing fancy. Thought he would get bored soon."

"I don't know what his intentions are. It's none of my business."

One was avoiding the details of a scandalous relationship, and the other was avoiding the details about Alois's indiscretion. Which of them was the worst for it? Jutta locked eyes on Katharina's. "Do you remember the day you needed an envelope? You were writing to the Ministry of Civil Engineering."

Katharina looked away, that dark shadow passing over her face again.

"What was that about?" Jutta pressed. "You told me you would explain it later."

"It was nothing," Katharina said.

"Did you write to *him*? Did you take the letter to Iris Bianchi and tell her about Annamarie's father?" She put a hand on Katharina's arm, but the girl went stiff under her touch.

Katharina's voice was flat. "I wrote for Opa." She pulled away, and Jutta's hand fell to her keychain. "It doesn't matter. It didn't work. We never heard back from the department." Her eyes darted towards Iris Bianchi. "I think we can do better."

"Do *what* better?"

Katharina faced her. "Recognising who we need to fight and

who we need to help. Right now Father Wilhelm needs our help, and if you need something to do, then do that. Excuse me."

Katharina went to the teacher and led her out of the *Stube*, leaving Jutta—amidst the room full of mourners—to stand alone.

Word had spread quickly about the discovery of the school. All week, and like mice in the dark, Jutta could imagine the sound of people scratching out hiding places for the banned books, wiping down the chalkboards with vinegar so as not to detect a shadow of a German letter scratched in, and salvaging the Bibles under stacks of hay.

When the *carabinieri* did come, when they insistently pounded on their doors, everyone held their breath. And if something was found? The rumours were already spreading, if only in half-uttered questions: "The Blechs know that their neighbours were sending their youngsters to Father Wilhelm. What if they..." "Thomas Noggler has a crush on that *Walscher* schoolteacher. What if he..."

Then there were the smugglers who had built up their part of the business in the school. Jutta sent messages to them and warned them to stop bringing in the latest books and newspapers from Germany and Austria. The Italian patrols would conveniently forget the bribe money that had been paid to them, she was certain of that, and if the contraband were found, even she might be arrested.

She went to a pile of papers on her credenza and found the one she was looking for, an article in the *Bozner Nachrichten* from last week. Two teachers had perished in prison after being convicted of running similar underground schools. The fine had been so high, the teachers could not pay it. Then there were books being burned and hearings held without proper representation or in the language of the accused. The tone of the article was flat. There was no outrage. There was no commentary. No gruesome details. It had been censored into a warning. Tell the people what was happening, scare them, and make them obedient. She understood that. What the Italians did not understand—especially if she had anything to do with it— was that it would eventually have the opposite effect.

She made the sign of the cross, put the paper under a pile of others, and finished pinning her hair up. She had to do something to stop the tide.

In the locked drawer of her credenza, deep in the back, was the envelope of money for Alois. She took it out and put it into her dress pocket, keeping her hand on it. In the hallway, she felt the emptiness around her. The door to the post office was still locked. Eric, the post-robbing Italian postman, was late again. Another night of drunken debauchery in the Italian quarter; at least he no longer lived under her roof. He'd stolen a bottle of her schnapps, and even the prefect had agreed to moving Eric out.

Down the street she could see workmen repainting the Prieths' bakery. Herr Prieth was watching from the window, his mouth turned down. The painters were stencilling in the Italian word *panificio*. Herr Prieth disappeared from sight when he saw her, and a workman looked down at her from his ladder. She scowled at him and hurried away.

There was nothing for it. They were creeping towards her, and the wall of the guesthouse would soon read *albergo*.

She reached the Farmer's Bank and waited. Hans should come at any moment, and when a few minutes later she saw him walking down from Arlund Road, her heart fluttered so much she could hardly breathe. It might work. It might not. She hoped it would. She hoped their friendship was strong enough for this. She called to him and met him at the corner of the building.

"What are you doing here?" he asked, cautious.

She glanced at the door of the bank. "It's today?"

He nodded.

"What are the chances that Federspiel can still do something for you?"

He looked away. "It's over. I can either sell it off, or they will have to auction it."

"Oh, Hans. When did you find out?"

"He warned me at the wake."

She lifted his hand and pressed the envelope of money into it. He reacted as if she'd burned him.

"Listen," she pleaded. "It may be enough. I've been saving it for years in case…it doesn't matter. I was saving it in case of an emergency. Take it, Hans. It may tide you over and you can keep the farm and then…just listen. And then whenever you can, just whenever you can, you pay me back, or you help Alois if he ever needs it. Maybe he could help you around the farm? It will be a way to repay me if he learned something."

He just stared at her.

"Why? Why not, Hans? What will you do otherwise?"

"I can't do that." He ran a trembling hand over his beard. "Unless?"

He had to take the money. He had to. What would Hans do without his farm, without his sheep and the wool?

"What is it?"

He looked regretful and swallowed. "It's not right to take money from you, Jutta. Unless…unless you were my wife. If you were my *wife*."

Jutta took a step back. She had expected this at some point, had hoped for it, but not like this. "Don't be ridiculous, Hans. I won't marry you so that you can have my money—"

He dropped his head and pushed past her. "I didn't mean to…"

"Hans!"

"I'm no good at this," he said without turning back to her.

"Hans! You can't give up! Just take it, for the love of God. Let me help you."

He finally faced her at the entrance of the bank. His eyes were shining. If it were not for his beard, she could tell whether he was crying or enraged.

Stupid pride! Stupid, stupid, stupid pride.

She marched after him, ready to shake it out of him, but Martin Noggler came around the corner, dragging Thomas by the ear.

"At least I don't have to go to school twice in one day," Thomas cried, and Martin walloped the back of his son's head.

She looked for Hans, but he'd melted behind the door of the bank. Protests from the churchyard came next, and she spun around. The *carabinieri* were leading Father Wilhelm towards the barracks. A small group of villagers followed behind, and someone shouted that the *carabinieri* were cowards.

They had found something of the school.

She made to follow them, paused at the bank window, and pressed the envelope of money up against the pane, but Federspiel had already put a fatherly arm over Hans's shoulder. With their backs turned to her, they withdrew into the shadows.

8

A ngelo was buried in the paperwork that was coming across his desk. They required his approval, or stamps, or signatures and attention. Much attention, more attention. Three bridges that were being built in Bolzano. The new roads up in Lana and Merano. Then the dams.

First, the Gleno Dam: An inspector's report about bad working conditions and concerns that the dam was poorly joined at its foundations. He would have to speak with the Colonel again about this. Saving money was one thing, but moving the completion of the dam to the end of November now was too risky. He paused and remembered the day he had asked Pietro about the new permits. He picked up the receiver and asked Mrs Sala to find the archived files on the Gleno. When he hung up, he turned back to the surveyor's report. At the bottom of the page, he wrote a note that he would later reword to the Colonel: *Get this into shape, or it will not be opened in time for the king's attendance. If I need to check on this myself, I will (where is the permit??).* Before laying the report to the side, he made a mental note to send his risk assessor down there.

The next one was from Stefano Accosi, his chief engineer on

the Glurns project: The workers had tunnelled into the mountain with very little incident so far. One small cascade of rock from a weak spot, but no injuries. In comparison to the Gleno, this was great news.

Kastelbell: Some of the landowners had put in new claims and appeals regarding the amount of compensation they'd receive. They were already unhappy with the agreements they had signed. Angelo had a pile of these, and they were tiresome. Pietro had warned him that stamping final approvals on things lulled one into a false sense of security; they were just the beginning of the real job. "And," Pietro had said, "that bigger mahogany desk you're taking over only means you'll be taking more work on, not spreading it about more thinly."

Angelo put the letter from Kastelbell on top of a pile of similar disputes. Then the letterhead from the Consortium for the South Tyrolean Waterworks stared up at him. It was a copy of the report they had sent to Rome. The Colonel's signature was scrawled across the bottom. He bristled.

Rome had promised Angelo that his proposal to raise Reschen Lake by five metres would be approved. Now the consortium was lobbying to raise it by twenty-two metres. Their report touted a lucrative production of energy for Italian industry. The more value for money would appeal to Rome well enough, save for the relocation plans of the citizens. Not dozens, but hundreds of properties would be affected.

Here they were again on the political carousel, but he was going to stay one step ahead of this manoeuvre. He rifled through the papers before him, looking for the soil sample order, when the phone rang. He lifted the receiver.

"Mrs Sala, did you find the file for the Gleno? And where is that work requisition for the Reschen Valley I asked you to draft?"

"I put the requisition with the other papers on your desk, and

I haven't got to the archives yet. Minister, before you hang up, Mr Michael Innerhofer is here to see you."

Pietro had once confessed that he would have preferred a dragon lady guarding the gate to the minister and scaring everyone off, but Mrs Sala was the widow of one of Pietro's work colleagues. Angelo wondered now if he would be able to do what Pietro had not and replace Mrs Sala with a tougher woman. Like Gina Conti. He liked that idea.

"Tell him to make an appointment with me."

She hesitated. "Sir, he did. Today is his appointment."

Christ. "Send him in." He stood up to greet Michael and recognised the suit, even more frayed at the cuffs.

Michael's dark eyes darted around the office, as if searching for clues and misplaced contradictions. As journalists, Angelo mused, are wont to do.

Michael's eyes landed on the table next to the bookshelves where the detailed model of the Reschen Valley was. Stefano Accosi had built the model to show exactly what areas would be affected. Michael drifted to it and examined it. He would see the mountain villages and the plans Angelo had for diverting the river. The reservoir would affect the edges of Reschen, Graun, and Spinn. It was a compromise, but the best Stefano and he had been able to come up with.

He strode over and gave Michael the stiff, quick handshake that indicated he was a busy minister and, therefore, in a hurry. "Take a seat."

Michael flashed an uneasy smile and sat. He reached into his breast pocket and pulled out his cigarette case. "Mind if I smoke?"

This would take longer indeed. Angelo reluctantly pulled the crystal ashtray from his desk drawer and placed it in front of the journalist, who was patting around his faded jacket pockets. This was the first time Chiara's acquaintance was interviewing him.

Chiara's friend. Chiara's accomplice. He did not offer Michael a light.

The journalist found his own, and when he had taken his first drag, he leaned back and scanned the office less discreetly. "Many changes, Minister. Lots of development. You are a busy man."

"Yes, I am. I'm pleased that you can appreciate that. How are things at the paper?"

"A constant tug of war with the censors," he said, his accent thick. "They check the advertising too now."

"Yes, I'm sorry to hear that." Angelo glanced at the report from the consortium and turned it over. To be polite, he should ask about Michael's family, ask how the brother, Peter, was doing after losing his teaching position. He was relieved when Michael cut the pleasantries.

"I'm not here to discuss my work troubles, Minister. I will write a story about the banks and the land they buy up. Your ministry is responsible for bidding on many auctioned lands, no?"

"Oh, I don't know if it's that many. We have the authorisation to purchase land as allocated within the projects, certainly, but you're talking about a matter between the landowners and the banks, not the landowners and this department. We get the information about available properties just as any other citizen." Angelo smiled and opened his hands. "We just happen to be in the market for a lot of real estate at the moment."

"You mind if I ask you questions? I want to get this story straight." Michael flicked the cigarette over the ashtray and raised an eyebrow. "My Italian, you see, is bad."

"It's become much better." He meant that sincerely.

There was a defiant look in Michael's eye. "You are too kind. But maybe I should ask you to speak to me as if I'm a child. Make sure a simple Tyrolean like me understands everything."

"What do you want to know?"

"How many more projects do you have in the frontiers? Coming?"

"The ones that you already know of. There are not many more."

"Not many more? What is *many* to the Italians? It's not the same for us Tyroleans. One is already too many. You see, it is relative. I need numbers. Mussolini has big plans, as does the new senator, Ettore Tolomei."

"Tolomei's speaking at the Municipal Theatre next week. He'll probably have many of the details you're looking for."

Michael narrowed his eyes, the corners of his mouth grim. "I look forward to meeting him face to face. Tolomei always had big plans for Tyrol. Big plans to make it Tyrolean free and wipe us off the face of history. Italian history, that is." He was referring to the Alto Adige as if it still belonged to the Austrians.

"Mussolini knows that here, we have money," Michael continued. "He marched on us last year in his big boots to see how much of it he could shake from the ground and see if we would run to leave it behind."

Angelo shifted in his seat. Indeed, in some ways the Tyroleans, this area, rather, were better off than almost the rest of the country, but he wouldn't describe it as rich.

Michael exhaled smoke. "I'm not talking about lire, Minister. I refer to the resources. Land. Water. Grain. Fruit. Wine. Borders." He sounded as if he were running through a grammar school vocabulary list. "All things that turn to gold for your prime minister."

The sooner you accept that he's your prime minister too, the better, Angelo thought. He said, "Do you not want your country to prosper? These developments are for the entire nation's well-being. I agree with most of what is planned and under construction, Mr Innerhofer, because it is meant to improve our standard of living. Add to your prosperity."

An irritated smile spread across Michael's face. "Our province prospered before you came. At the cost of our landowners, no, Minister, we do not want to see more of it. Tolomei is, what is the word? A python. He squeezes us around the middle, and departments like yours have their hands around our necks. But allow me to get to the facts." Michael flipped open a small notepad and read, "The number of forced foreclosures and auctions of farms with loans at the Farmer's Bank increased tenfold in the last year. It is in direct correlation to two things: the projects coming out of this ministry and the bank's new board of directors, made up of only Italian members." He looked up, earnest. "I've prepared, but please feel free to correct my grammar if you still hear a mistake. I would hate to offend anyone's Italianism."

Loathsome man! Angelo cleared his throat. "Go on."

"Your ministry decrees new roads, new bridges, new dams, everything new, to bring in more Italians from the south, and you buy off property cheap so that you don't have to pay compensation, even restitutions, later." He looked up, his pencil poised over a blank page now. "These lands have belonged to the Tyrolean people for hundreds of years, many generations. Over and over, these families live, work, sweat, have families in these houses and on these lands, and in less than one year, you swoop in like...like crows to shiny things and exchange them for contracts they cannot understand because they do not know the language." Michael held a hand up when Angelo shook his head. "How many more projects, *Herr* Minister? How many more projects with no regard to people on those lands and around those lands?"

"I am not at liberty to tell."

Michael nodded, drew in a deep, smokeless breath, flipped his notebook closed, and stubbed out his cigarette. When he finished, he looked up, his smile complaisant. "I think I have a grasp on this language of yours. You say you agree with most of what's being done. Tell me what you do not agree with."

"Nothing comes to mind."

"Chiara says to me that you're unhappy with the Reschen Valley project." He turned slightly towards the model. "She says you stand against it."

Damn it, Chiara, Angelo thought. He'd mentioned it to her once. Once, when he'd had a tirade about the Colonel's plans, and she had been sympathetic. Maybe she was even ignorant about how Angelo felt adversarial towards Michael, but no matter what her intentions, she was not helping matters one bit by opening her mouth. Not to this man.

"To an extent, I do not agree with it. Not all of it."

"What does that mean?"

"I, myself, proposed to keep the original plans that the Austrians had outlined. It would provide enough electricity for the intentions decades ago." He leaned forward. "The reservoirs and dams are necessary. You can see for yourself the industrial growth we have, and that calls for more electrical power."

"But the Reschen Valley plans are in dispute, no? Chiara says Rome is greedy and even you are concerned about, how do you say? The impacts. But who has the power to make decisions, Minister? Rome is not listening to you. The consortium is not listening to you. Who *is* listening to you?"

"You're out of line, Michael. I am not the one you should be angry at."

Angelo pushed himself away from his desk, itching to put this man in his place once and for all. "I get my directives from the legislature. On the rare occasion from Mussolini himself. I can only make my recommendations and appeals based on the surveys and the expert reports. Yes, my power is limited, but what I have available, I use to the fullest extent."

Michael laughed drily. "Limited powers, you say. Interesting. The consortium's president is Colonel Nicolo Grimani, your father. Your father runs the growing electrical *Monopol*: Grimani Electrical. Limited powers because you are, what is the phrase? In cahoots. You have an interest yourself to see the Colonel's success. After all, you do have a son, an heir."

Angelo stood up and leaned over his desk. "I can assure you that I do a clean job." He winced inside. Glurns. Kastelbell. But he'd been sure to cover his tracks. "There is nothing you can write that would prove otherwise."

"I only write the truth."

"Here's the truth, *Herr* Innerhofer: the world does not give a damn about a little valley in the outback of *Italy*. After the war and when all the world's politicians drew up the treaty, not even the US president checked the maps he'd received. Tolomei and his delegation drew the rivers to run from south to north, and nobody came to investigate if *that* was true. The world's leaders *wanted* it to be true because it was a matter of convenience. The Americans were not about to dispute the agreements in a pact drawn up by the Triple Entente and Italy in nineteen fifteen. Tyrol, south of the Brenner Line, was sold out. And *that*, Michael, *that* was a big deal. *That* redrawing of the maps and the geography—of *history*—that part of the Versailles *peace* treaty attracted national attention, and nobody gave a flying damn about truth then. Nobody paid attention to the fact that you are all German-speaking citizens with a different culture, with a different language and history and that, *that* alone, compromised Woodrow Wilson's ninth of fourteen points. Now..." He shrugged. "You and the Ladins, of whom no one has ever heard, are Italian. So, *Herr* Innerhofer, I ask you once more. Why should anyone in power want to be inconvenienced? You will soon see that you too are limited by the system."

Angelo stalked to the window located behind his desk and caught a reflection of himself. The black hair swept back, the beard he had grown making his face fuller. He could not see his eyes in his reflection, just two dark shadows where they should be. Michael was busy scratching in his notepad. He decided to let the journalist catch up. It did not matter anymore. Let the censors deal with him.

When Angelo focused outside the window, he saw the street where the parades took place and the church. He saw carts of hay being lugged by barefooted boys, and wicker cone baskets filled with early apples on the backs of old women. He thought of the Reschen Valley. He thought of her. Of Katharina.

Turning back to Michael, he pointed out the window. "The electricity we will get and the compensation we pay will put an end to crumbling houses and farms in a mountain province where prosperity now means that someone owns more than one pair of shoes. The world will see this dam as *progress*.

"Why *wouldn't* the Reschen Valley people be happy to accept recompense or sell their land for a better life? Mussolini's government is offering money or a steady income for land that will be of some use to necessary and modern changes."

Michael's face was satisfactorily stony, and it provoked Angelo to continue, even if he did sound like the Colonel. "Progress! That's what this is all about. This ministry is doing all it can to bring advantages to *all* its Italian citizens as intended. You included."

Angelo sank back into his chair and turned the consortium's report over. Beneath it was the drafted order for new soil samples in the Reschen Valley, ready for his signature. He looked up at Michael, to share the document as proof that there was nobody leading his ministry by the nose, but Michael was at the door.

"Thank you for your time, Minister."

"Michael, I *am* trying to do things right. I cannot stop progress, but I can help with the impacts and make sure they are safe for the citizens. You can quote me on that."

The journalist pursed his lips and shrugged his shoulders. "The Italian citizens, you said. And those of us who are still in no-man's-land?"

"Tell me. I really want to know. How do you propose to get this story through the censors?"

"Did you not hear? We are being pulled into the river. It won't be long now."

Angelo did not understand.

"Tug of war," Michael said. "The last two Tyrolean papers will go under, *Der Bozner* and *Der Tiroler*. Tolomei is making sure of that. We are losing. I am free to work for whom I want."

"Around here, Michael, that too will be limited." His tone was regretful enough.

"You mean to say you are sorry to hear it. You notice, *Herr* Minister, how you always apologise for the things that are too late to change?"

Angelo was reading an opinion piece about the German Worker's Party when Chiara walked into the salon. He wanted to address the visit with Michael, reprimand her for convincing him to do the interview, but she had Marco in her arms, and as soon as the boy saw him, he squirmed to get down. Angelo placed the paper aside and lifted his son onto his lap.

"He wanted to say good night to you since we missed you at dinner," Chiara said.

Angelo kissed Marco on both cheeks, and his son snuggled into him. "Let him stay." He turned back to his newspaper to finish the last lines, then asked Chiara, "What do you think of the situation in Germany?"

She was sitting on the settee across from him, her eyes on their son. "You mean the growing anti-Semitism? The blaming of all the wrong people for the treaty's unfairness? I read that article, calling on Hitler to march on Munich like Mussolini did on Rome."

Someday he would learn to stop having these discussions with her.

"He's tired," she said.

"Hitler?"

"Your son." Her voice was softer when she spoke again. "They ought to be watched carefully. Hitler seems to follow Mussolini's path, like a little brother imitating his big brother."

"Uh-huh." He reached for his *Journal of Civil Engineering*, careful not to disturb Marco.

"Edmond believes his party's nationalistic fight is the right one, but Susi sees through it," Chiara said. "She says she doesn't like the smell of it."

"Really? How quickly the leaf turns. The great divide between the count and countess has grown more than just geographically, I see."

Marco's head jerked, and Angelo lowered the journal to look into his son's face. The boy's eyes were closed.

"I'll put him to bed." Chiara stood and hovered over them.

Angelo touched her wrist before she could take Marco from him. "Michael came to see me today."

"He said he had."

So she'd seen him afterwards.

As she scooped up Marco, he put a hand out to her, but she kept her arms around his son. He picked up the newspaper from the table and held it up, the anger rising so quickly it came out in his voice. "Tell me how we can keep the outside world away from us, from my family."

Chiara's face read surprise, and she pressed Marco to her. "Obviously you're as interested as I am in the way things are progressing. Neither of us is in a position where we can keep these things *out*, Angelo."

"Chiara, it isn't who we are. We did not come together as man and wife because we wanted to change the world. I want peace in my house. I want peace between us. I want my *wife* back."

"I have always been here. I never went away. *I* have not changed."

A bright, sharp sliver raced from the back of his head, over his scar, and pricked his breastbone. He had to look away from her.

"Funny how little peace we have now that the battles are over," she said. "The war was just the start, wasn't it? You have served your country to come this far. You serve it now too, I suppose. You're right, Angelo. We did not come together as man and wife to change the world. We came together *despite* the fact that we have been involved in changing it. This *is* me, Angelo. I have always taken an interest in justice and in people's rights. If I remember correctly, it was what fascinated you about me in the first place. And you. Well, do you know what side *you* are on? Do you know what *you* really want?"

He watched her jawline move as she waited for an impossible explanation. She wanted a black or white answer, right or wrong. In all her experience with politics, *with people*, did she not realise that she would never get that kind of answer from him? Or anyone?

She sighed and straightened with the boy in her arms. "I see no difference between living with a wolf in sheep's clothing and a lamb dressed up as a wolf. None at all."

Wednesdays were market day, and the air was saturated with jasmine. On the way home to lunch, Angelo walked through the square, when he passed Signora Conti at one of the flower stands. She was wearing a close-fitting blue hat or he would have recognised her sooner. He looked around. Neither General Conti nor any of the four children were to be seen. Her tunic-shaped dress was the colour of crushed pomegranates and only hinted at the curves beneath. He had seen her often, heard her speeches often enough, but he knew little about her save for what others said, or from the rumours that swirled around the general's wife. Her many male admirers in the party had not gone unnoticed by Angelo, yet she appeared to be loyal to the one castoff amongst that crowd: General Conti. Perhaps the rumours were just indecent fantasies.

The florist was putting together a bouquet of roses and gardenias for her when Angelo stopped next to her and pretended to admire the flowers. After she paid, she turned and recognised him.

"Minister Grimani, what a pleasure."

"Signora Conti." He raised his hat and kissed the hand she offered him.

"It's a fine day to buy flowers," she said. "Your wife will certainly appreciate some. The roses here are exquisite."

She was different, this close and this unguarded. Sweet. Accessible.

"Perhaps Signora will help me to choose the most beautiful one then."

Her smile was obliging. "It depends on what you would like to evoke with them. What would you like to say to her?"

"I am afraid I have not thought it through," he said. "The prettiest rose and the one that will last the longest will do." He'd not bought Chiara flowers in probably over a year, and the realisation was a jolt. He had better explain himself. "You see, we have plenty of rose bushes around the villa."

"I understand," she said. "You are frugal as well. I'll not bore you with romantic nonsense then. As an engineer, you will want something straight, well built, and functional."

"And beautiful."

Her grey eyes flashed amusement. "Of course. An engineer who is also interested in aesthetics. These days, a rarity indeed."

"You sound as if you are unhappy with the modern architectural style."

"Ah, but you are not then?" She smiled before looking down at the buckets of roses. "Allow me to find the rose that represents you just as well."

She sifted through the flowers, sometimes checking whether he approved. Her face was smooth and heart shaped, and when he watched her move in that dress, he thought again of pomegranates, the globe-like fruit with its tough rind, the chambers he had to fold back to get to the meat. He pictured his thumb running over the seeds to loosen them from the piths. Sweet, succulent. And he never got a mouthful without staining his hands. He could feel the lust that had emerged on his face and quickly masked it.

"This one," she said, holding a coral rose. She reached for another one, a dark ruby red. "Or the classic. Would you like to know the difference in their meaning?"

Was there a colour for *if my wife won't have me, you'll do just fine?* "I don't have to know. They are both straight, well built, and functional, as well as beautiful." He paid for them and held the coral rose out to Gina. "Signora, if you will allow me, you were immediately drawn to it, and therefore this one is for you. My wife prefers the classics."

"You ought to know what such a rose means." Her eyes were fixed on his, long lashes a little lowered. "I couldn't accept it."

Angelo smiled apologetically, confident of what he was about to start. "Of course not."

"But I will." She gingerly took the rose from him and handed it to the florist. "Add this to my bouquet please. Place it right in the middle." She turned to him. "That way I may always keep an eye on the minister's delightful gift."

The florist obliged her, and Angelo imagined the flowers in a vase on the Signora's dining table, hiding the sulking General Conti behind them. He could also picture her in the ministry, those legs across from his desk every day. When Signora Conti had the flowers in her arms again, he offered to take her shopping bag and walk with her a part of the way.

"This is a rare pleasure, Minister."

"You must cease calling me Minister," he said.

She smiled at him and touched his arm lightly with a gloved hand. "What should I call you then? You are the minister, and Minister is such an appropriate title, isn't it? Besides"—she laughed softly—"I can't call you Senator. Not yet anyway."

"Of course. I apologise, Signora. The formalities do not allow for anything more familiar."

Gina smiled broadly. "Oh, we can change all of that, can't we? After all"—she wrapped her hand lightly around his forearm and leaned into him—"we are comrades in arms. That's where I prefer the Socialists. They are all so informal with one another and call one another by their first names." She laughed softly, grey eyes steady, watching him.

He gave her an acknowledging nod, and Gina suddenly stopped. They were standing outside the Laurin Hotel, and she tilted her head towards the entrance.

"Shall we tread on more familiar territory, Minister? Or are you in a hurry to get home to your family?"

Angelo checked his pocket watch. Either way, he would already be late. "Perhaps an espresso at the counter."

Gina moved ahead and led him through the lobby, the smoky saffron window behind the reception desk casting too church-like of a glow for his tastes. The hall echoed with the footfalls of people coming and going, of knives scraping against porcelain, and the soft murmur of people tucked into their luncheons and conversations. Next to the reception desk was the spiralling staircase that led to the rooms above. He fantasised leading her up there, but the idea of it was as far as he would let himself go.

They went into the café, and at the bar, she ordered two Martini Biancos. He watched her scanning the lounge and looking at herself in the large mirrors where the drinks and wines were written in white chalk. The hotel was gilded in every shade of yellow possible: lemon, gold, brass, saffron, and sand.

The dark wooden tables, the rust-and-white chequered floor, and the grey marble countertops were practically the only contrast. And Gina.

"It might be awfully naughty of us when we know lunch is waiting at home," she said. "And at midweek. But I'm very glad we are finally talking. We frequent the same places, and I hear so much about you, but we never *talk*, do we?"

She turned and leaned against the bar, her elbows barely reaching the top. For a moment, he thought she might kick her legs up, like a showgirl. He had the distinct desire to remove her hat, unpin the dark hair underneath, and watch the black waves cascade down her neck and shoulders as far as they would go. He could understand how someone would easily misconstrue her intentions. Or be fascinated by her. She excelled at walking the thin lines of leader and follower, disciple and rebel, matron and sex object.

The barkeep placed the glasses of aperitifs on the counter, and she tipped hers towards him. "Are you back from your daydreaming? Or do you really want an espresso?"

"I'm sorry. No espresso. To your health." He drank while she eyed him over the rim of her glass. "I have many things in my head. Work, that is."

"I heard that you're sending out for soil samples to the Reschen Valley."

He caught his reflection in the bar mirror, his surprise unmasked, his disappointment just underneath. Was the game over and she would turn to business? "I did not realise it had already been made public."

"Minister Grimani, the state is absolutely pleased by every step in the right direction. Such news cannot be kept secret for long, especially amongst such indiscreet zealots as you have working in the ministry." Her eyes flitted over his face, and she laughed. "Don't look so horrified, Minister. I am only joking. My cousin works with your testing team. He was at my mother's seventieth birthday party last weekend and told me he had to go up north. I told him he is working for a good man."

Angelo relaxed. "I didn't realise I work with relatives of yours."

She chuckled and took another sip from her martini. "We Italians have become gypsies, flocking north to see the world. But it's dull here, isn't it? The Tyroleans and old Italian settlers are already such good, stoic Catholics, Minister. Such solid, upstanding citizens. If I tried to talk to the Tyrolean women up in the provinces about the duty of womanhood, I would be preaching to the choir."

"Where would you rather be then?"

"Now, that, Minister, is not the right question. Not where I would rather be, but where am I most needed? Do you know where I am needed? I mean really needed?" She smiled over her glass. "Paris. Berlin. London." She raised her glass and clinked with his. "The news trickling down from there is that there are no practising Catholics left and no decent women in those cities. Just bohemians and Communists. A true Sodom and Gomorrah." She seemed to relish the words. "That's where I am needed, Minister. I'm afraid I will just waste away here. You see, I've converted the most important women involved in the suffrage movements and the socialist movements except for...well." She raised the drink to her lips, but her eyes landed on the red rose on the bar. She placed the emptied glass on the counter and turned to him. "Let's get ourselves home to our meals, shall we? Or we'll lose ourselves in the idea that we *are* in Paris and need absinthe to get through our days." She patted her hat and winked. "We have our reputations to keep, you and I."

Head spinning, and not from the spirits, he paid the barkeep and escorted Gina to the door. For lack of anything else to say, he thanked her for her help with the rose.

"We must do this again, Minister." She brushed a gloved hand over his arm. "More often."

She went right, and he went left, turning once in time to see the flash of crimson before she disappeared around the corner.

He backtracked to the florist.

"What does the coral rose signify?"

The woman blushed and finished wrapping a bouquet for a customer. When they were alone, she said, "Lust. Desire."

Angelo lifted his hat and gave her a few coins.

Dangerous as a forgotten fire in a dry summer. That was Gina Conti.

At the villa, he already had his hand on the doorknob before he turned around, went to the garden at the back of the house, and stuck the red rose in one of the bushes.

The sun had not yet come over the peaks of the Rose Garden range when Angelo took his breakfast on the veranda. Saturday was just another working day for him these days, but today was a right horrible mess. He put a wool blanket over his shoulders and poured himself a coffee from the silver carafe. The china jangled as his hand shook from anger or lack of sleep, or maybe both. He balanced the cup on the landing as he looked out at the vineyard below, the grapes finally taking on fuller form. He heard sparrows arguing, and a crow cawed somewhere behind the house. As the first rays of dawn reached the valley floor, he saw the insects take to the vines. Below him were the white oleander bushes his mother had given them last year.

His father was coming later, to meet with him and Pietro. Angelo considered cancelling. He needed time to prepare. To analyse. To sleep and gather the strength necessary to keep the Colonel in check, especially after last night.

Angelo rubbed his forehead and slapped his thigh. "Damn it! Where *is* she?" She was at Susi's of course. He meant, why wasn't she home yet?

He turned his thoughts to last night. Chiara and he had gone, arm in arm, to Senator Tolomei's rally. It was the first time since he had accepted the ministerial position that she had gone with him to a political event. Still stinging from her calling him a sheep in wolf's clothing, he had hoped that by going together, they could form some sort of public allegiance. *Look at me, Minister Angelo Grimani, on the arm of my progressive wife. We* both *have an interest in Italy's unification. We are the ideal couple, working together.*

It had been a mistake. He should have just given her the rose.

What was supposed to have been a harmless speech by Tolomei became a nightmare. The theatre had filled up, not with people from Bolzano, but from specially chartered trains from Trentino. Senator Ettore Tolomei reenacted the Bolzano Fair of 1921 and Mussolini's march on Rome. When Chiara also realised who was showing up to Tolomei's rally, she had looked at Angelo as if he were hand feeding her to her feared wolves. Only when they had found her friends in the crowd had Chiara regained her composure.

Then instead of giving a speech about how he appreciated being made senator, Tolomei introduced a thirty-two-point measure for the eradication of German culture in the Alto Adige. Before Tolomei had even finished, the theatre erupted into a thunderous ovation save for the drowned-out booing of Chiara and her progressive comrades planted about in the wings.

"I hope you're happy now, Minister," she had said to him, her arm long gone from his. "Tolomei is about to clear the path for you and the Colonel. The Grimanis will have a new street named after them in every major town."

She had left with Susi, Peter, and Michael, and she still was not home. He pictured Michael. Dark, sullen, intelligent, and distant. A visual victim to an oppressive government with his frayed cuffs, his newspaper articles and notepads, his cigarettes and hazy smoke. A romantic hero in the making.

"Damn it," he cursed, and two birds burst out of the oleander bush.

As if she were right there, Angelo suddenly heard Katharina's voice teasing and shy.

"Damn it, Herr Grimani. Damn it. *Die ganze Zeit nur*, damn it." Always with the damn it. Despite himself, he chuckled, surprised by the fondness. By the wrenching twist to his heart.

Why was he thinking of her now? He glanced at the breakfast table. Angelo's copy of *Popolo d'Italia* was folded neatly next to the breakfast plate. He sat down, cracked his egg, cut off the top, then opened to the front page of the paper. Tolomei's photo was right in the middle, with his grey handlebar moustache, the dark eyebrows over scholarly spectacles, daring someone to contradict him. It could be said that the former inspector general of schools and well-known nationalist had single-handedly obtained the Alto Adige for Rome, and now he was going to finish Italianising it. All the points from last night were listed on the next page. Trentino would become the capital of the Alto Adige. The Italian borders would be closed to those whose Italian citizenship had not been conferred. Chiara's friends would officially have to register themselves as Italian if they wanted to travel to their relatives north of the border, because one of Tolomei's points was that visitors from Germany and Austria would have Tolomei's hurdles to jump in order to obtain visas.

Point seventeen decreed the removal of the statue of Walther von der Vogelweide from Walther Square in Bolzano. Angelo snorted. Tolomei was not missing a thing. How was that going to do anything other than make the Tyroleans feel degraded? Well, there was his answer. He kept reading and remembered how Michael had turned to him, giving him a curt nod: point nineteen introduced measures to facilitate the purchase of land, and immigration by Italians. Next, an extensive railroad infrastructure construction program connecting rails from the south with those of the north. Increased troop strength. Tolomei had finished by encouraging foreign countries to maintain a policy of noninvolvement in the Alto Adige.

"Tug of war, Michael, was it? And you're losing indeed, but keep my wife out of it." He put the paper down and closed his eyes.

Only after the sun had seeped over the veranda's railing did he hear the sound of a motorcar. He leaned forward to watch the taxi pull away. Chiara was home. Finally. In the hallway, he heard Marco's laugh and turned in time to see him running down the hallway towards the front door, his nurse right behind him.

Chiara came out onto the veranda sometime afterwards, redressed for the day in a soft beige and dove-grey skirt and tunic. The colours made her look paler despite the colour she'd put on her face, but her red hair had been freshly combed back. Even if she looked tired, she was far from finished.

"Why?"

"Why what, Chiara?"

"Why do you allow yourself to be a part of this? A part of the Fascist's agenda? You can't possibly back Tolomei's measures."

"I don't. You know that."

"Then why?"

"Because after spending time with them, it makes me feel like a better person."

She laughed, a short, mirthless laugh, and took her seat at the breakfast table.

"Tea or coffee?" he asked her. "I'm afraid I have to ask for something fresh. They're both cold."

"No sleep?"

"Like you."

She nodded and twisted her egg cup. "I don't want anything."

"You have to keep your strength up."

"You have a meeting today, with our fathers, about all the appeals coming in on the projects."

"Yes."

"Solutions?"

He shook his head.

She pushed the egg to him. "Then it's best you eat it."

He reached for her hand, still on the egg cup, and managed to touch her before she slowly pulled away from him. *Were you at Susi's, Chiara? Or at Michael's?*

"You must be tired," he said.

"Our anger kept us going."

"I was worried. The whole night. You could have telephoned." He waited for her to apologise.

She stifled a yawn. "Cristina and Francesca are coming with your father. We are shopping for a present for your mother. It's her birthday tomorrow."

He had forgotten. "Would you like me to make the excuses for you?"

She looked out on the garden below towards where his sisters would be coming. "I really see too little of them."

Angelo sighed. "Family, Chiara. That's all we have in the end. Just the family. The rest of it does not matter." He eyed her and waited for her to look at him. When she did, he said, "Have you thought about it? Us having another child?"

She picked at something on her skirt, then looked over the veranda again. He imagined her trying to conjure up his sisters, and he felt a bitterness rising in him like bile.

The breeze ruffled the loose top of her tunic. "I'm taking Marco with me," she said. "To the shops."

He acknowledged that he'd understood.

She looked at him. "I worry that it just would not be right."

"What's not right? To give Marco a brother or sister? That our family continues to grow?"

"To bring another child into the world now."

"There is never a right time," he snapped.

"There is, Angelo. There is a right time."

"Fine. Then we can be careful." He leaned forward. "I want my wife, and I don't want to wait for a gold-leafed invitation to her bed."

Her face rippled with different emotions, and for the first time in a long time he saw her really looking at him. He waited for her to say something flippant, to straighten up and lash him with her liberal diatribe. He waited. She said nothing.

"I have done everything," he said, "to keep this family together. I work hard for you, for Marco, for your parents. I aim to make the best of a bad situation. I have not denied you anything. Not your new outfits. Not the new furniture or the things you buy when you are sad or upset. I have never ordered you about. Tell me how many husbands would make the allowances I have?"

He stood up, and she jerked back in her seat.

"Stop it," he said. "Stop treating me as if I were some sort of monster. I understand. You do not agree with my ways. Now accept that I know what I am doing and that what I am doing is in the best interest of my family. I'm the minister of my department now. I give the orders. Do you understand?" He stared at her pale face. "Goddammit, Chiara, it's time I put my foot down."

Over the landing, he saw his sisters and the Colonel coming down the street. Chiara saw them too and rested one hand lightly on the landing.

"I'm coming to you tonight, Chiara. I expect that you will open the door to me when I come."

She raised her chin but did not turn to him. "Your wish, Captain? Or your command?"

He left her there, her eyes still on the street.

9

GRAUN, SEPTEMBER 1923

The cuckoo clock in the *Stube* read a few minutes before eleven in the morning when Jutta heard the doorbell ring. She finished wiping down a table before dropping the rag into the bucket just as the hanging bell above the front door clanged. Hadn't she locked it?

Emilio Rioba and the two *carabinieri* he never seemed to be without, Vincenzo and Ghirardelli, stepped into the dining room. Of course. Rioba still had a key. His policemen had the same look dogs do before being released on a hunt.

"*Buongiorno*, Signora Hanny," he called.

"The kitchen's closed on Tuesdays."

He took off his fez and looked around the *Stube*. "*Cambiano i suonatori ma la musica è sempre quella.*"

She squared herself against him. "I know that you speak my language. Tell me what you want."

Rioba sighed and placed his cap back on his head, then gestured to the other two. Ghirardelli hesitated a moment, gave a respectful nod, and he and Vincenzo turned on their heels to go back into the hallway. Jutta moved to follow them—they had no business in her inn—but Rioba held up a hand, blocking the way.

"*Prego*, Signora. Stay here." He looked around. "No guests?"

"I told you already. We're closed on Tuesdays." She had two geologists from Munich, and they had the necessary permits to be here. She didn't care who Rioba was or that Ghirardelli had just been assigned as police captain. They had no right to harass her customers. She stared the prefect down.

In any other world, Rioba might have been a nice man. The curly black-and-grey hair, the distinguished features, and the intelligent eyes gave the impression of a pleasant man. He was also very fit for his age. She had often seen him walking the hills early in the morning. The days when the Italians were their summer guests and had gone climbing with people like Johi Thaler as their guide, those days were gone, but she could imagine Rioba being one of those *Sommerfrischler*, then coming back to the inn, refreshed, rejuvenated, hungry, and sitting down to dinner with his family with enough energy to play with his grandchildren. If he even had a family.

From the kitchen, she heard something crash to the floor and shatter into what must have been a thousand pieces. Rioba raised his eyebrows before Jutta shoved past him and to the kitchen. The policemen were sorting through her porcelain and throwing each and every piece onto the tiles. In his hands, Vincenzo, the small, squarish brute, held her mother's handmade water pitcher. He sneered, lifted it above his head, and slammed it to the floor. It shattered like an egg, liquid and shell. Behind her, Rioba murmured something reprimanding, but it sounded false in her ears. Ghirardelli looked at least sheepish, like a naughty schoolboy, as he destroyed her expensive serving platter.

In his hand, Rioba held a stack of the postcards that Jutta kept at her front desk. He fanned them out, their backs right side up. His tone was the one she used with Alois when she had to explain, repeatedly, why she was denying him something.

"No German, Signora Hanny. Forbidden. No *tedesco, capisce?* We have this discussion before. No signs in German. No

114

dishes in German. No postcards in German. No maps in German. *Solo in italiano. Siamo in Italia.* We are in Italy."

Jutta clenched her fists into her skirt, her keys rattling. "I *did* remove everything. All of the crockery: for the honey, for the salt, the hot water, the lard, all of it." Everything except her mother's pitcher, which she rarely brought out of the cupboards, but had today because it was Tuesday. Nobody came on Tuesday.

Rioba clicked his tongue and cocked his head. "And the postcards?"

"These just came in. You blackened the old ones last time, and they were all sold."

"Sold or thrown away?"

She gritted her teeth. "Sold."

Enrico was behind this. He must have ratted her out to Rioba about the new cards. She looked at the shattered dishes and the mess the police had made.

"Do you know how much these things cost me?" she demanded. "There was not a single German word on those plates and platters. Nothing is marked on my crockery."

Rioba clucked his tongue and gestured to Ghirardelli, who was holding a lone, whole porcelain plate. When he had it in his hands, Rioba turned it over and pointed to the blue inscription. *Augarten. Wien. Österreich.*

"*Tedesco,*" he said. "This is German writing. German language."

"This is outrageous. You're destroying all of my porcelain because of a stamp on the bottom of the plate?"

The prefect scanned the kitchen floor and shrugged before handing her the last plate, undamaged. "Signora Hanny, I send you a catalogue for porcelain from Capodimonte. They are Napoli's finest. *Cosa molto belle.*" Rioba smiled, "*Va bene?*"

"How dare you!"

He made a slight hand gesture, and his two dogs abandoned the kitchen through the back door. "Rules are rules; orders are orders," he said. "In *italiano* we have a saying—I said it when we started—the melody has changed, but the song remains the same. Signora Hanny, it is time you learn that song."

He straightened his fez and followed his men out.

"What on earth happened?"

Kneeling amidst the debris, Jutta looked up to see Katharina shift Bernd in her arms and Florian leading Annamarie away from the shards.

"Rioba" was all Jutta managed.

Wordlessly, Katharina and Florian helped her sweep and pick up the shattered crockery and porcelain, the noise as grating as fingernails on a blackboard. Jutta put her mother's water pitcher into an empty apple crate. Three chunks formed a good half of the pitcher with "Cold Water" painted in her mother's hand whilst the rest was a shattered garden of yellow, blue, and red flowers. Katharina kneeled next to her, and Jutta kept her head down, raising her hand to wipe her brow so as to catch the tears.

Sometime later, Florian said, "We're finished here."

Jutta had barely moved from the spot where they had found her. When she looked around, the kitchen looked in good order save for the empty dish racks.

Katharina led her into the *Stube*, where Florian was now opening a bottle of wine. She dropped her face into her hands. Annamarie whined about something to her mother.

"Is she hungry?" Jutta asked behind her palms. "There are some rolls in the kitchen."

When she heard a glass placed before her, she took her hands away from her face to drink. "I'm glad you came."

"This is worse than what they did to you in the summer," Florian said.

Her voice shook as she told them the details. "They're

hounding me. They think they can suppress me, but they're wrong. I've survived a lot worse than them."

"What will you do about the dishes?" Katharina asked. "There isn't a single plate left for tomorrow."

Jutta shrugged. "I'll borrow some from the Adler's guesthouse or hang a sign on the door for everyone to bring their own." She was the only one who smiled. "Forget about me. How's Hans? You'll be bringing the livestock down from the *Vorsäß* soon?"

Florian nodded. "Next week, we think. The weather's been holding up fine."

"And he'll be living with you then?"

"It will take some adjusting for Hans, more than for us," he said.

Katharina nodded. "He's grieving. It's only natural."

"It's a shame," Jutta said. "A horrible, horrible shame. I should have been more insistent about taking the money." She had never told anyone about Hans's marriage proposal in exchange, that marrying her would have been the only way he'd have accepted her savings.

Katharina patted her hand. "Don't blame yourself. You did what was right for you, and there is nothing to regret there. You helped Father Wilhelm when he needed it. If you hadn't paid that fine, he may have been taken to the prison in Bolzano."

"But the bishop repaid me, you know that. The church would have taken care of him. Hans was the one who could have used that money to save his farm." She should have accepted his terms.

"God has his ways," Katharina insisted. "You were saving it for Alois, and now you have it back for Alois. Hans will be fine with us. We extended the barn for the animals he's got left. He'll just start over. Like we have."

Katharina glanced at Florian. "Besides, it's good timing to have Hans with us. The little that he can pay us in rent and the rent we're getting from Florian's mother's house will help us to pay off the bank. And then we can get the deed. Right, Florian?"

He nodded, but his mouth was drawn.

"So you have decided not to sell the house in Nuremberg," Jutta said.

"I can't. With Germany's inflation, I'd lose money. Besides, we might need the house someday."

Katharina frowned and picked at something on Annamarie's dress.

It was the thorn in Katharina's side, Florian's talk about moving to Germany. "It's better than losing the Thalerhof," Jutta said.

Florian shrugged. "That's relative."

"For you," Katharina said sharply. "Tell her, Florian. Tell them what the bank offered for the farm."

Jutta stared at both of them in turn. "You wouldn't sell the Thalerhof, would you? What would Hans do then?"

"No," Florian said. "I won't. The offer was low, and Dr Hanny warned me not to do anything rash."

"Now you don't have to," Jutta scoffed. "With Hans's help, you should be fine." Her anger towards Rioba and the two *carabinieri* flared again. "Whatever these Italians try next, I'm done being agreeable with them. It's time we give them a taste of their own medicine. We stick together from here on out. If we do that, we can beat them. It's them or it's us. Not like Frederick."

"What do you mean, not like Frederick?" Katharina's tone was challenging.

"With his engagement to that schoolmistress," Jutta cried.

Katharina bounced the baby, looking annoyed. "Iris is a lovely person."

"She signed the document that blocks my son from getting an education."

"Where is Alois, by the way?" Florian asked.

"With David Roeschen. They took the goats up to the pastures this morning." To Katharina, she continued, "That schoolteacher has blinded Frederick. That's all part of their plan, Katharina.

Marry our people and start reproducing Italians." She looked at Annamarie. The girl was watching her. Jutta picked up her glass and drank.

Bernd began to cry, and Katharina stood up, her face stony. "Jutta, you really don't see it, do you? There's a better way. There is."

"I suppose you're going to tell me again that we should all learn Italian."

Katharina looked at Florian once more, but he was studying the ceiling. "We have to protect ourselves," she said, "and in order to do so, we have to learn the language. We can't ask or demand things if we can't communicate and reason with them. It's the only way any of us are going to keep our land."

Jutta sat up straight. "My dear child. What has got into you? Your grandfather's Opa fought with Andreas Hofer for our self-determination, Katharina. Take this law now, with having to tie up your dogs. Hund's a cattle dog, for heaven's sake. First they threaten to shoot our dogs, and then it will be us. Do you want to be like Hund, Katharina? Tied to the lead of the *Walscher*?"

She waited, but both Katharina and Florian were mute. "You two, of all people, owe that to Opa. You owe it to the Thaler heritage, to Tyrol, for heaven's sake, to stand against the people who are taking away everything that makes us who we are." She slapped a palm on the table, the sting satisfying. "You don't reason with tyrants and the devil. You fight them."

"All right." Katharina's voice was strained. "Then remain ignorant and let the authorities pull the land right out from under you. This inn"—she jabbed her finger on the tabletop—"that you fought so hard to own. For heaven's sake, Jutta, if I even had a chance…"

"Katharina," Florian warned.

"What? It doesn't bother you that we don't have a deed yet, because you have a house in Nuremberg. What about me? It was supposed to be my farm."

Florian took in a deep breath, and Jutta looked from one to the next.

Katharina sat back down, staring at the table while Bernd bounced more furiously on her knee. When she looked at Jutta again, she was glaring. "And if you think the attorneys are going to help any of us, well, Frederick—the brother-in-law you feel you must renounce—is the one who warned us that our own people are pocketing bribes, then turning around and convincing their neighbours and supposed friends to sell out. If we don't understand the contracts and allow the Italians to do what they want to us, we will have nothing left to defend and nobody to blame but ourselves. We won't be able to blame Mussolini, not Rioba, and certainly not the Ministry of Civil Engineering when they decide it's time to flood our neighbours' fields."

Jutta jerked back. "What did you write to Angelo Grimani? You know something, don't you?"

Katharina shot out of her chair, and Bernd exploded into shrill cries. She grabbed her daughter's hand. "I'm going to get those rolls for the children." She threw Jutta a cold, hard look before dragging Annamarie towards the kitchen.

Jutta slumped into her chair. She wouldn't be able to take back what she'd said. Not this time.

Florian's question was on his face. "What has Katharina got to do with the Ministry of Civil Engineering? It keeps cropping up. Who's Angelo Grimani?"

She was imagining what Katharina might have written, remembered that Katharina had gone to Iris with the letter, but not to her. "Johannes Thaler and the others were talking about writing to the ministry personally."

"So what's Katharina got do with it?"

She shrugged and glanced at the *Stube* door. "No idea. I assume she just knows about it." She gasped then. "Wait a moment. There's a soil testing team, arrived from Munich two days ago. Said the ministry ordered them together with a testing team from Bozen. If the German geologists can confirm the original tests, then certainly the ministry will foresee the problems with the soil."

Florian pursed his lips. "I guess."

If so, then maybe it was Katharina who was responsible. Maybe this Grimani was a valuable asset.

Jutta finished her wine and stood up to get the bottle from the bar. She returned to pour Florian a glass.

"I have another question," he said as she poured.

She looked up.

"Who was the man Katharina was in love with? Before I came along? Was he from around here? Because she has nothing left to keep her here that I can think of, and yet she resists the idea of moving to Germany with all she can muster."

Jutta steeled herself. She handed him the glass and sat down, her eyes steady on his. "She has the Thalerhof, Florian. And her kin buried here."

"And Annamarie's father. Who was he, Jutta?"

Her heart tripped in her chest. "I didn't know him. He was just passing through, stole Katharina's heart, and now he's long gone." She wasn't lying.

"Was he an Italian? Admit it—if you look at Annamarie, she could be Italian."

"Florian, let sleeping dogs lie. I mean it."

"I would," he muttered, "if it weren't for the fact that people always meet twice."

"That won't happen, Florian." God forbid. "He was nobody. Nothing to her."

"And the man that was stabbed by Fritz? There was a connection, wasn't there?"

"I told you, I don't know."

Florian looked off, shaking his head. "I'm taking my family to Germany, Jutta. This Hitler and the NSDAP, they make sense.

They have good ideas about how to improve the economy." He shrugged, "After all, I have a homeland too."

"Your mother was Tyrolean. Florian, we need you here."

His smile was sad, and there was an edge to his voice. "Jutta, you once told me I'd never get to the bottom of all the secrets in this valley. You said there'd be a lot more to cover up before I could dig up what's underneath already. I'm not interested in secrets, and this valley seems to thrive on them. I've been forthcoming with you folks. I want to be a part of something where I know whom I'm dealing with. These Italians are bringing out the worst in us instead of the best."

He stopped, and she felt as if she could cry.

"Who is this Grimani, Jutta?"

"It's not my secret to tell, Florian."

"I saw Katharina's face, Jutta. You already did."

10

GLENO DAM, NOVEMBER 1923

A ngelo and his men drove through the countryside, entering the scattered villages of stone huts, all swept clean and decent in anticipation of the king's envoy. Each time the locals heard the car, they waved and cheered, only to be visibly disappointed that it was just Angelo and his crew within. It kept his men amused on the long road to the Gleno Dam.

The pylons that marched from the mountains down into the valley reminded him of huge giants with outstretched arms. Angelo remembered a game he'd played as a young man, where he and his friends would create two fronts—arms linked, one team standing opposite the other. They would chant a verse and call a name from the opposite team, and that person had to run with all his strength into the opposite line with the goal to break them apart. That was what the pylons reminded him of now, a team of giants waiting for their opposition.

When the car breached the ridge after Bueggio, he leaned forward to take in the dam's arches. He could imagine the king's speech already, referring to it as a monument to Roman culture, Roman tradition, Roman strength. Even from this distance he could see the walkway had been decorated in red, green, and white banners and streamers, with the black flags of the Fascist party.

"The roads are good, Minister," his driver said. "His Majesty should have no trouble getting to the ceremony."

Angelo had his eye on the wall, but when the water appeared behind it and he saw its level, he turned to his chief engineer in the back. "Stefano."

"I see it," the man said. "Heavy rains from five weeks ago."

"See to it that you talk to the watchman. I want those levels checked."

Stefano nodded, and Angelo turned back just as they approached the gate. The guards let them through, and Angelo stepped out of the vehicle, the Colonel on his way to them. The board members of Grimani Electrical and the politicos were already being served glasses of *prosecco*.

He pointed out Barbarasso to Stefano. "Ask him to find the watchman for you."

Just as the Angelo's father approached, Stefano made his way over to the former lumber baron, now the Colonel's right hand.

"Angelo." His father formally extended his hand, then pulled him in for a kiss.

"Congratulations, Father. Sorry we're late."

His father grimaced, glancing over Angelo's shoulder. "We? Need I remind you that attending these events without your family is not going to help your political career? Why aren't Chiara and Marco with you?"

"You didn't really expect them."

"Never mind," the Colonel grumbled. "His Majesty and the Queen are delayed by an hour or so."

"Hurry up and wait," Angelo muttered.

"What's that?"

"Nothing." He was already moving along the dam's walk to see the water for himself and removed his hat to bend over the rail, when he heard Gina Conti's laugh.

She and the general were just leaving their car, Gina already being greeted by one of the board members. Since the last time Angelo had seen him, General Conti's hair had thinned and greyed, and his posture bent forward as if he were caving in on himself. Next to him, Gina stood out in a wine-coloured cloche and a fox coat. He suspected that style was less important to her than the colours she wore: always bold, always resplendent like ripened summer fruits or Christmas ornaments. Either way, it was a far cry from her sombre Fascist outfit the first time he had seen her, or her military-like manner on the day she'd called women to join the party.

Whereas the general seemed to stay where he was, Gina was on the move again. She attracted the Grimani Electrical board members like iron filings to a magnet, while repelling their wives, as they often took a step or two back when she came near. She hovered over one man then the next, leaning on one arm, touching another, and always laughing. Drunk on ability.

He thought of the day they'd had martinis at the Laurin. Angelo felt a stirring, like a near slip off a cliff. For her, he might just jump, save for the fact that Gina would be a woman he would never be able to get rid of. The aftermath of his affair in Arlund had been nothing like that. Which might have been his salvation thus far.

The general had drifted to the railing on the reservoir side, and Angelo wondered what the Contis' home life was like. Perhaps it was her husband who grounded Gina after an exhausting day of weaving intrigue. Angelo could picture her, calm, not talking, not smiling, not beguiling. For General Conti would not notice anyway, and Gina was not one to waste her energy on useless matters. On the contrary, at the dinner table, adjacent to the general, she'd be accessible, even vulnerable. She might coax him to take a spoonful of soup, but with that same motion, she would be plotting her next move.

She was now at Luigi Barbarasso's elbow, who may have

dominated her in both height and girth, but looked the fool with his wolflike grin and obvious fixation with her. She outranked him in poise and composure. Since Angelo had become minister, he'd been privy to her affairs, the details of which dribbled out with other secret agendas after a long night of wine and spirits. One thing was certain—Gina Conti could either help a man or hurt one, and she used the same network to accomplish either.

She moved to the Colonel, but her eyes were suddenly on Angelo, and the way she smiled and the way her eyebrows tilted up signalled that she'd caught him watching her.

Stefano moved between them, having returned with a tall, humble-looking man in tow, and introduced the watchman.

"If you are on the first shift," Angelo said to the man, "the king will hand the keys to you after he's cut the ribbon."

The watchman thanked him for the honour, but looked nervous. Stefano encouraged him with a slight nod.

"Minister," the watchman said, "I have been meaning to talk to someone at your agency. I warned Signor Barbarasso about the heavy rains. The reservoir is almost filled up completely, yet he insists that we open the gates tonight."

"We will have a word with the Colonel."

"I don't wish to go behind the backs of my supervisors," the watchman said.

"I understand. We will keep it discreet. It won't come back to you." He pulled Stefano to the side to give him instructions, but his eyes landed on Gina as she slipped away from the group of men and picked two glasses of *prosecco* off a waiter's tray.

"Minister, so good to see you again."

She handed him one of the glasses and kept the other, tilting her head at Stefano in mock disappointment as she raised her glass. "My apologies. I only have two hands."

Angelo nodded at his chief engineer. "I'll find you later."

When Stefano had left, Angelo clinked glasses with Gina.

"I hope I didn't interrupt anything serious."

"I'm afraid I have to check on something. In the end, it is me who is responsible that everything is up to par."

"Yes, I had almost forgotten about your obsession with details." She indicated the walkway of the dam's wall. "But not your love for aesthetics. It is beautiful. Better to look at from above or below than here, but the dam is beautiful. Powerful." There was a flash in her eye. "What were you thinking when you were watching me?"

He was ready for it, her direct manner. He realised with a start that he'd been looking forward to another chance just like this. "You seem to be the designer of your very own web. That is what I was thinking."

Gina laughed, her head tilted back, but her eyes never strayed from his face. He felt that thrill again.

"Are you saying I am a spider? I suppose I have heard worse." She moved so that they were standing side by side on the railing, on the side that overlooked the deep gorge. "I like the idea," she said, "but only of the spider web, not the spider."

"No? Why the web?"

She chuckled. "You men all think the women are black widows. Dangerous. Feasting on you. It's a cliché. The metaphor of the spider is not about the sexes, Minister. It is about where you are on the food chain."

"What do you mean?"

She became contemplative. "There was a summer night many years ago. I could not sleep. It was hot. And there was a clicking sound outside the window, like someone flicking at their fingernail. It kept up into the morning, and so I went down to the balcony, where the noise was coming from. I looked for the source, and finally, in the corner near the door, I found a small beetle, no bigger than this." She pressed her thumb and forefinger together. "It was very small, you see, but it had a hard shell and was trapped in the remnants of a spider web. It had gotten itself terribly twisted, almost cocooned. I was amazed that such a tiny thing still had the energy to keep fighting. Its will to live was impressive."

"And the spider?"

"I found it crouched under the doorframe. It seemed to be waiting, as if it was terrified of coming too close before the beetle had tired."

"Did you not release the beetle?"

She smiled. "That would be against nature, would it not?"

"So it died."

"I never went back to look. I didn't need to. You see, Angelo, I was never inspired by the spider. On the contrary, I often feel like the beetle, surrounded by things that want to suck me dry." She turned ever so slightly to the group of men behind them. "But they cower in the corner, afraid of what it is my will can do."

He felt that rush again. "And am I one of those spiders, waiting by your entangled web?"

"Oh, no, Angelo. Like me, you are the beetle." Her eyes landed on the Colonel before she turned back to him. "Except with you, the spider has already inserted his fangs. "

He was off guard, his laugh proof of it, but her eyes stayed on his, grey and sombre. Like he'd imagined she would be with the general.

He closed his mouth.

The sight of the empty champagne bottles sharpened the pain in Angelo's head, and his hand went to where he'd find that scar from the attack. They were as much a part of him as anything, he supposed, the scar and the attack.

Angelo dipped into her cigarette case, and Gina stirred from sleep as soon as he flicked on the lighter. He watched her fingers snaking their way to his cigarette. He inhaled once and handed it to her as she sat up, propping her pillows against the headboard.

Cold winter sunlight sliced diagonally across their saffron-coloured sheets. He was numb.

"It's my birthday today," he said.

She exhaled and handed him the cigarette back. "Today is—"

"December the first."

"How old are you?"

"Young enough for you and old enough to know better."

"I'm good for you." She opened the black lace robe, exposing her body. Her hair fell over her breasts, and he let his eyes rove over her curves.

"Just yesterday," she purred, "you bowed to the king, and today, I will make you feel like one. Happy birthday."

He sat up and swung his feet to the floor. His wallet was on the bedside table, certainly much lighter after all the bribe money he'd paid to the Laurin's porters. Bribe money and champagne. He stood up.

"What's wrong, darling? Where are you going? I offer you what your wife won't, Minister, and you turn away?"

Angelo halted but did not face her. "There were two things you agreed to in this hotel room," he said measuredly. "One, you do not talk about my wife."

Bed linens rustled, and when Angelo looked, Gina had jerked the sheets over her nakedness, looking defiant and amused all at once. "Yes, and two, no titles and no lovey-dovey nicknames. And I agreed to much more, Angelo, much more." She snapped the covers off and exposed the inside of her left thigh, tracing a finger over his bite mark.

He had cracked her open, and it was easy to understand how Gina Conti ticked. She did anything, drove him to do things he didn't think he would. He remembered how Luigi Barbarasso had ogled her at the Gleno opening.

"And your other liaisons?" he said, striding into the bathroom, but his tone was one of a jealous boy. "Do *they* like to be called by their titles?"

"Most of them like to be called Prime Minister, but, darling, if you want to keep eating at this table, let us agree that *you* are not allowed to ask *me* such questions."

He rubbed the beard around his mouth, then punched a hand into the basin of water and washed. He was being ridiculous, behaving like a love-struck schoolboy. He should stride back in and make love to her again. He was supposed to be gone the entire weekend. Nobody knew they had returned to Bolzano.

"Besides," Gina said, "*Il Duce's* year as prime minister may be finished, but nobody is going to ask him to step down. You will all have to give up on the dream of being his successor."

"Madonna." Angelo whistled, beard dripping. "Who the hell wants that job now?"

Gina chuckled. "For now, that is. But Angelo Grimani as senator? That might be interesting."

His heart jumped as if it were playing hopscotch. Senator? That would rile the old man. Imagine making laws, he thought, that would hinder the Colonel...

From the mirror, behind his dripping face, he could see Gina reclining, her body only visible to him up to the midriff. Behind the door, he heard her light another cigarette, and she exhaled loudly. A plume of smoke wafted from where her head would be.

He watched her slowly raise one knee. Damn it if he didn't forgive himself and just get back in there.

"It's Saturday," she said, followed by an obvious yawn. "And your...they don't expect you back until tonight?"

Chiara believed he was still up in Bergamo. And the general had left Gina alone to attend an important meeting the next day. It had all been too easy, and he felt uneasy about that.

Angelo dried his face, his armpits, and the rest of him, then stuffed the towel into the brass ring. "This weekend is a one-off, doll," he said with as convincing an air as he could. "Then it's over." It had to be.

When he was at the edge of the bed again, she smirked up at

him and stubbed out her cigarette. She kept her eyes on his as she opened her robe, unfolding her legs one at a time. The woman who made men.

"Then," she purred, "you'd better take all you can get."

Later, there was a light knock on the door. Angelo dressed himself and threw the covers over Gina, sleeping again. "Who is it?"

A voice behind the door said, "Sir, it's the porter."

"We didn't call for anything."

"There's been an accident. I…I thought you should know."

Marco. Chiara. Angelo whipped the door open. "What's happened?" It was the same man from late in the night, or early that morning.

The porter lowered his eyes. "There's been a dam break. In Bergamo."

"The Gleno?"

"Yes, sir. They're saying the whole Povo Valley is flooded."

Angelo was moving, left the door open. He didn't care what the porter saw now. "Gina. Get up. You have to go home. There's been an accident."

"Who? What?" She was up and dressing like a soldier called to a raid.

"It's the Gleno Dam." To the porter, he said, "When did it happen?"

"Early this morning."

"Jesus," Gina said.

Angelo fumbled in his wallet, his mind racing. The watchman. The water levels.

The porter waved his hands when Angelo handed over the money. "That won't be necessary, Minister. We can handle the bill later. And Signora Conti, sir, she may take her time."

Without another word, Angelo followed him out into the hall and had him hail a taxi. Behind him, Gina called but then the door swung shut.

At the ministry, the corridor on his department's floor was filled with people hurrying, waving papers. They greeted him in hushed tones and sideways glances. Angelo pushed past them to his office, where he startled Mrs Scala, on the phone. She looked as if she'd been crying.

"He's here. He's just come in," she said into the receiver.

The clock read twelve past ten. She hung up the phone. "Minister, we've been trying to reach you and have looked for you everywhere. The hotel in Bergamo—"

"Call the consortium together, my surveyors, and the Colonel."

His risk assessor walked in. "Minister, we're all in the conference room. Waiting for you."

Angelo ran a hand through his hair and followed his man. "Brief me."

"Six thirty this morning, the buttress of the dam cracked and subsequently failed. We're estimating that about four and a half million cubic metres of water spilled out into the valley within minutes. The rains—"

"Yes, I know. The elevation above sea level is just over one thousand five hundred, is that right?" He started calculating.

"That's correct, sir. They estimate that there was a breach of about eighty metres in the central portion of the S-shaped planimetry. The village of Bueggio was flooded first."

Angelo had booked his hotel nearby until Gina had seduced him, had convinced him to return to Bolzano. She had said that they would be safe at the Laurin. Protected, was the word she had used.

"Damn it to Christ."

"Minister?"

"Sorry. Where are the maps?"

"Just here, sir."

They moved down the hall towards the conference room. Two men were holding the corners of the map up on the wall and conferring over it. They stepped aside for him.

"Continue," he said.

"Dezzo is partially flooded." The risk assessor's voice betrayed his stress. "And Azzone as well. I'm afraid that the flood propagation along the downstream river were catastrophic. It took the flood wave about forty-five minutes to flush through to as far as Darfo."

Angelo shook his head in disbelief. "That's over twenty kilometres."

The assessor swallowed. "Three villages and five power stations have been completely wiped out, sir."

Chills rippled down his whole body. "Are our people accounted for? Our chief engineer, Stefano? And all the others who were at the opening?"

The man swallowed. "Some left, the chief engineer among them. He's here in the conference room. Others were staying the weekend. We thought you might have…"

Angelo felt his eyes stinging. "Jesus, Mary, and Joseph. Christ!" He paused at the door of the meeting room. He saw Stefano, and Pietro was also in there, as if ready to take charge again. Angelo knew all the people in that room. He knew every single one of them, and he turned to look down the hallway because the Colonel was missing. The doors swung open at the end of the hall, and there he was, in military dress. He too had left the area then.

When he reached Angelo, they looked gravely at one another before Angelo turned to the risk assessor. "Casualties? The numbers?"

The risk assessor glanced nervously at the Colonel. "Umm, sir…we are still calculating—"

"I'm aware of that." Angelo would fire the risk assessor later. He held his father's gaze. "What's the number so far?"

"Over two hundred, Minister."

"Right. Order the car. We're going there as soon as we're finished here." To his father, he asked, "Army mobilized?"

The Colonel nodded. The risk assessor hung his head.

Angelo opened the way into the meeting room. "We are keeping this meeting brief. You're both coming with me."

"Stop the car," Angelo told the driver.

They were trapped behind a convoy of military trucks trying to make it up the icy road. He, the Colonel, Stefano, and the risk assessor stepped out onto the road some ways away from the dam break. Stefano started taking photographs. Angelo saw that the road was about a dozen metres lower than it had been a few days before and pointed it out to the Colonel. He went to the edge and nearly stumbled backwards. Below him, the valley had been laid to complete waste, the walls of the canyons scoured by the water. Some of the pylons were twisted, the lines dangling like useless, broken limbs. He could make out the debris piled upon a black muddy bed that was now the valley. Not far below him, a horse lay on top of a cart, angled and bent in death. Against the rock wall below, four dead goats.

"Give us the field glasses," Angelo said to Stefano.

Stefano put the camera aside long enough to fetch the glasses, and when Angelo had them, he adjusted his, then made sure the Colonel was lifting his set to his face.

Angelo eyed the risk assessor. "Stefano, have him take the photographs." He glared at the man. *Let the bastard see what his bribe payments had paid for.* "You, keep your hands from shaking."

Angelo lifted the field glasses and scanned the valley. The first thing to come into view were the piled-up trees, then the flattened wooden boards of houses that had once stood on stone foundations. Those foundations were nowhere to be seen. He scanned the floor and saw what looked like a body of someone on a trunk. He looked closer. It was a naked man, slumped over a chest that had lodged into the mud, the water over the man's ankles and wrists, the body limp and grey-blue. He heard the Colonel make a guttural noise and looked over to where he pointed. More bodies, this time a woman and two children twisted amongst a debris of trees. Above them, like a world on its head, a straw mattress.

The water had already begun receding, but Angelo could imagine the snake of mud carrying carts and houses, the bodies of people and their animals slithering through the valley. A wall of water, someone had reported, a wave as tall as ten or fifteen houses had preceded the mud. He could imagine the sound of it, like a cyclone or a hundred locomotives. He lowered his glasses.

"This may be the greatest engineering failure of the century," he said.

The Colonel pointed farther north. "The bridge is washed out over there. I don't know how we'll get to the Gleno."

"Did you see the bodies?" Angelo asked.

The Colonel's face was twisted. "I've lost most of my men up there. Some electrocuted by the very lines they were trying to protect."

"Down there," the assessor interrupted. "Look. Someone's still alive."

Stefano grabbed the camera from the shaken man and pointed it to where the risk assessor had been looking. A unit of soldiers was making their way down into the valley, but then Angelo saw what the assessor had. Three people were slogging through the water and mud, without a stitch of clothing on them, and this in December. They were sifting through the piles of debris. He heard the sound of the camera again and again, and then the Colonel's voice.

"Does that man of yours have to take so many photos? What on earth does he hope to get from this perspective?"

Angelo itched to tackle his father off the road and feed him to the black snake below. "Goddammit, Colonel, he's documenting our wake-up call."

~

"Three hundred and fifty-six deaths, that we know of," Angelo said to Pietro. He lowered the report.

"It's good that we're meeting at your office," Pietro said. "We must keep things official, not personal."

"I've ordered a full evaluation of all dam designs for projects in progress," Angelo said. "And, Pietro, we're doing it my way. I won't take any more orders from the consortium or any private companies until we've had a chance to assess all of this. I want a full overhaul of our risk assessment departments. I warned you, years ago, about the reports coming in, about the sloppy work, and it just slipped out of control as soon as we allowed the Gleno to go private."

Pietro sighed and shifted in his seat. "On some points I agree with you, Angelo. Money had a lot to do with it too."

"Money? Let's start with the bureaucracy. For Christ's sake, Pietro, it took us how long to get the damned second permit? They changed the whole structure before they even had it. Talk about putting the cart before the horse."

The phone rang, and Angelo lifted the receiver. "Is he here?"

"Yes, Minister."

"Send him in."

Pietro stood up and turned towards the door. The Colonel came in, looking ready to do battle, white gloves in hand, but Pietro took a step forward and gave him a careful embrace.

"Nicolo, we're all here as concerned citizens, and as family. Let's remember that."

Angelo stepped from behind his desk and gave the Colonel a brisk handshake. When they were all sitting, he corrected Pietro. "Today's meeting is strictly a department matter. You're here to consult. And you"—he eyed the Colonel—"are here to get a summary of our findings."

The Colonel whipped his gloves against his thigh once, then stuffed them out of sight.

"I have the watchman's report here," Angelo said.

"That he survived," the Colonel said, "is a miracle."

"It was luck. He was at the other end of the dam. We already had concerns about the water levels, as you know, at the opening. Especially after all the rains. On November thirtieth, he called my risk assessor, but my man assured him there was nothing to worry about yet."

"Thirty-eight metres," his father said.

"Correct. The dam broke the next day at seven oh five in the morning. About fifty minutes later, the last wave was reported in Darfo, at the end of the valley. According to the watchman, the buttress collapsed very fast—he guessed thirty seconds—and in three stages. The eleventh spur fell first along with the two arches resting on it, followed by spurs eight to twelve and then four to seven. Overall, a breach of about eighty metres."

He handed copies of the report to each man, summarizing the rest. "Subsequent technical examinations have proven that the collapse was triggered by water seepage at the interface between the masonry base and the overlying structure. *Your* structure, Colonel, for which we never issued permits.

"Many aspects have contributed to the failure of the multiple-arch dam, but ultimately the blame lies on poor workmanship. The concrete arches were reinforced with anti-grenade scrap netting." He waited until the Colonel looked up from his copy. "Anti-grenade scrap netting? I find that to be rather remarkable considering that you complained about those materials when we were on the battlefield."

He took a deep breath before continuing. "The worst of it was that the dam was poorly joined at its foundations, and evidence of poor masonry was also found. This along with those accumulated rains created perfect conditions for the disaster." He paused, certain to have the Colonel's attention. "We also heard from people who worked under Barbarasso. They claim that he fired anyone who complained about poor construction techniques. Secondly, my men were eventually on your payroll, lining their pockets with your bribes."

The Colonel remained unusually silent.

"What findings does Grimani Electrical have at hand?" Pietro asked.

His father grimaced. "If we have to pay for all the damages alone, the company will be insolvent."

Angelo steepled his hands. His father was not going to get out of this that easily, but there would be no more dams for Grimani Electrical for quite some time. He would get concrete numbers later.

"I am going to make changes to how we do things." He opened a folder and placed two documents before Pietro and the Colonel. The men leaned forward to read them. "One report is from the Geological Society in Munich, from a Richard von Klebesberg. He conducted the original geological tests and soil samples of the Reschen Lake decades ago. Then again about three months ago."

The Colonel looked up, and Angelo flashed him a warning look to let him finish.

"The report reiterates von Klebesberg's original findings. The soil is too porous. If you build a reservoir there, you'll create a wasteland when the waters recede. In other words, the valley floor will become a desert, and with that wind tunnel the valley creates, the sediment will spread and cover the remaining crops."

"But this one here…" the Colonel pointed to the second page. "This one contradicts that report."

"Yes, it does. The samples sent to Rome by my geologists have come back stating that the ground tests are clean. There could not be a more ideal spot for Grimani Electrical's next dam."

He heard Pietro suck in his breath. "That was not a wise move, Angelo. Does Rome know that you ordered samples to be conducted by German geologists?"

Angelo frowned. "No. And why should they?" He eyed the Colonel. "I want to know what I'm up against if I'm to do the job you got me in here for."

"That's treason, Angelo," the Colonel threatened.

He shrugged. "Then report me."

His father leaned back, looked at Pietro, and found no accomplice there. "What are you planning to do next?"

"I want to appeal the permit for the dam in the Reschen Valley. The one your consortium managed to get." He held up a hand when his father began to protest. "I know how vital it is. I've read all the reports, and we've been discussing this for years."

"Debating is more accurate."

"Come here." He stood up and went to the table where the model of the Reschen Valley was. The Colonel stood a distance away from it. "You see this?"

"You forgot the third lake," the Colonel muttered.

Angelo allowed himself the satisfaction that his father was sulking. "Come now, Colonel. Even the engineering department in Verona is against your plan. Their damage reports match mine, and I still don't have a good answer about what we'll do with the people living here and here." He pointed to the hamlet of Spinn and the outskirts of the two larger towns. The Italian officials' barracks, ironically, would be right on the reservoir's shore.

Pietro stepped forward and swept over the northern area of the model. "With your plans, Nicolo, all of these hamlets and villages would be wiped out. Even the higher ones, like this one." He indicated the model of Arlund.

Something stuck in Angelo's chest, and he felt dizzy. The nightmare, the valley floor rising with water, his despair. The panic washed over him, then receded. He went back to his desk. The other two followed him and took their seats again.

He addressed the Colonel. "You can't move almost two hundred grain farmers to higher ground and hope they can restart on the mountainsides. We're looking at one hundred percent losses to farmland and ground for livestock. Verona has doubts they'll be able to skirt the laws on this."

His father scowled and reached into his breast pocket. When he had his black notebook out, he took the pen from Angelo's desk and said, "Verona has a problem with my plans, you said. Who would that be?"

"What are you going to do? Have him fired as well? Or reeducated? The man is already a Fascist."

His father scratched something in the notebook, closed and bound it, and said, "Noted."

Pietro looked at the Colonel sideways before leaning towards Angelo. "There is a lot at stake here, son. Ordering geological reports from Germany could truly be seen as treason if you put the results into the appeals. What you are proposing—what you said before Nicolo came in—would mean holding up projects that are already in progress. Consider the costs."

"Oh, I am." Angelo smiled for the first time in weeks. He swept a palm towards his father. "I'm thinking about the well-being of companies just like his. I'm thinking about the long-term impacts on the economy."

"Angelo," the Colonel barked. "Geological reports have been wrong before."

Angelo pretended to take his warning seriously. "That's correct. They have been. Now you also understand why I intend to take careful precautions."

"What exactly are you proposing to do? Pietro, what did he tell you?"

"Father." Angelo leaned his elbows on his desk and looked him straight in the eyes. "I am proposing that you clean up your mess. Get through the hearings in one piece. Take a break. And then reinvent yourself. You're not going to convince anyone of your projects right now."

The Colonel looked as if he had just been punched, but Angelo wasn't finished with him yet. "In the meantime, I will rehaul this department before it gets out of control. That's not what I'm proposing to do. It's what I *have* proposed. And before you interrupt me, you could try and replace me with someone else who is sloppier, more in your pocket, but..." He pulled out his trump card: the directives, signed, sealed, and approved. "The prime minister himself has already sent me this."

His father stared at him in disbelief, but Pietro had the start of a smile on his face.

Angelo spelled it out for his father. "Mussolini has granted me full power to do as I see fit with your clean-up, Colonel. Gentlemen, for the time being, we're finished here."

11

ARLUND, APRIL 1924

Hans's oxcart rolled past Arlund's wayward cross, slush and snow piled on the sides of the road. The basket at Christ's feet was still filled with dried musty flowers from last autumn. As Hans steered his ox down the curve towards Graun, Katharina stretched out in the hay in the back, Bernd and Annamarie next to her, and looked up at the sky. Her daughter copied her immediately, her smile checking for approval.

"Look, Annamarie." She pointed to the clouds above them, changing shapes in a wind they could not hear or feel. "That one looks like an eye. Do you see it?"

Annamarie grinned and put two fingers to her eyes. "*Occhio.*"

"That's right: eye. *Dov'è il tuo naso?*"

Annamarie put a finger to her nose, and Katharina grabbed her hand and kissed it.

From up front, Hans greeted someone and reined in the ox. She sat up to look over the edge. It was the Ritsches.

"*Servus*, Kaspar. *Servus*, Toni," she called.

They lifted their palms to her and came to the side of the cart. "Just saw Karl Spinner," Kaspar said. "He got news from Germany that Hitler's on trial. Doesn't look good."

Toni spit snuff on the ground and scuffed his heel in the gravel. "Mighty disappointing. After that Beer Hall Putsch, we thought he stood a chance."

She glanced at Hans, but his face gave away nothing. Karl Spinner. Georg. The Ritsches. Even Florian most times. They all talked excitedly about Hitler and his politics, as if it had something to do with them. To her, Hitler seemed to be as much a fanatic as Mussolini. Just because he was German though, Hitler's politics were acceptable to these men.

Toni jerked his chin at her. "Going down to see Jutta?"

She knelt back in the hay. Actually, it was Iris she was meeting. "Hans is. I have to see to some things in town."

The Ritsches took their leave, and Hans got the ox going again. Bless him, he never said a thing about Jutta and her. Katharina kept her distance these days. She and Jutta simply did not see eye to eye on things, and she was careful what she shared with her, especially after Jutta's indiscretion in front of Florian. Most recently, Katharina heard rumours that the reason she was avoiding Jutta was because Katharina was jealous about her owning the inn whilst the Steinhausers were still waiting for the deed to the Thalerhof.

That hurt Katharina more than Jutta's slip of the tongue.

At the church square, Katharina helped Annamarie down, and Hans told her he'd pick her up in a couple of hours to take them back home. She headed for the Foglios' butcher shop, where Iris said she would wait after school. Aloud, Katharina was used to calling the butcher family by their Italian name, but in her head, she always thought of them as Blech-Foglio.

She walked in, the little bell ringing on the door, and the scents of smoked meat and garlic were just underneath the smell of the bleach Mrs Blech-Foglio used to keep the shop spotless. *Not a drop of blood on that woman's hands*, Jutta used to whisper when they'd walked in together.

Behind the glass case was a tray of dried horse sausages, piled

143

up on one another into an elongated pyramid. There was a hunk of *Speck*, with thick strips of fat, and another one with more flesh than fat, which was what Katharina preferred. Behind the butcher counter was a pork leg in a wooden contraption that Katharina had never seen before, like a skewer stuck the long way in a vice. The rind held a faded blue stamp, but she could not read it.

From the stairwell that led to her room, Iris called cheerfully, "*Come stai*, Katharina." She had Sebastiano by the hand, the Blech-Foglios' youngest. "I'm so glad you're here. It's a nice day for a walk. Sebastiano can come with us and play with Annamarie."

Katharina kissed Iris on the cheeks, then warmly linked her arm with Iris's. "It may be the only way we can talk about your wedding in peace."

The children were the same age, but Sebastiano was a little shorter than Annamarie.

Iris reached for Bernd and took him into her arms, smiling and kissing his cheeks. Bernd's face crumpled and, just as quickly, recovered in an uncertain smile.

They stepped out into the spring air and turned for the lake, but Katharina stopped when she saw Rioba in the square. He was standing over one of his official's shoulders, who was tacking something onto the wooden announcement board just outside the church.

Iris raised an eyebrow and tipped her head. "It will be in Italian, but I'm here. Let's go see the news."

"Let me try and guess what it says," Katharina said. "I want to see how much I can manage on my own."

Iris agreed, looking pleased, but Katharina first waited until Rioba had adjusted his fez and returned with the man and the hammer to headquarters. Anything to avoid him cheerfully chucking Bernd under the chin, calling him Benito, or commenting on how beautiful her daughter was, or something about Katharina's Italian.

Iris walked up first and began reading, and Katharina started with the headline. When she read the words *Ministerio il Genio Civile*, her eyes flew to the bottom. Angelo Grimani's name and a neat signature were there in black and white. Her heart pounded so much she was certain Iris could hear it and see it coming out of her chest.

"Katharina, you need my help?"

"No, Iris. No. Let me." The words swam before her, and she scolded herself for being so affected. It was an announcement for the whole community, not a private message for her from Angelo. She read the sentences and strung the words she knew into something that might make sense. They were going to stop the dam. She felt out of breath. Behind her, she heard Jutta's voice calling to someone, probably Hans or Alois. "Iris, it's about our lake. Tell me, are they putting a stop to the reservoir plans here? It says something about the Gleno too."

Iris had a curious look on her face. "Katharina, you wrote to this man once. I remember." She pointed to the announcement. "Was it a protest, what you wrote?"

"Tell me what he...what it says."

Iris switched to German. "It says that, especially because of the Gleno Dam break last year, the ministry is holding back all projects. They have to, *come se dice*...review? *Sì*, review safety ways. How to build the dam, *capisce*?"

They looked back at the tacked-on sheet.

"So," Katharina said, "nothing is going to happen?"

Iris shrugged. Then a slow smile spread across her face. "You did this?"

"I'm afraid not. It was the accident at the Gleno that caused this. Not me."

He'd never written her back. She'd often wondered whether he'd ever gotten the letter.

"The men from Munich were here, remember?" Iris said.

Then likely Angelo had indeed received her plea. "And the soil testing team from Bolzano," Katharina thought out loud. She looked at her daughter, playing with Sebastiano near a mound of snow. "So it's over."

"I think so." Iris smiled.

"I should tell the others about this." Katharina looked over at the garden of the Post Inn. Jutta was standing at the back gate, her hands on her waist, watching them.

"There is your *compagno*, your ally," Iris said. "We can go tell her now."

Jutta jerked her chin in their direction, straightened, then slowly raised a hand in a kind of greeting.

Katharina lifted hers in return. She missed Jutta, but how could she bridge the distance now?

She turned back to Iris. "Maybe later."

"She will never be happy to see me, eh? My future *cognata*, my sister-in-law."

Katharina took Iris by the arm again and leaned into her. "Don't you worry about that. Let's walk to the lake. I'm here to talk about your wedding plans, not problems with in-laws."

She took one last look at Angelo Grimani's name and then at Annamarie, who—with Sebastiano—was throwing dirty clumps of snow into the melting puddles to make them splash.

Next morning, the sky was a bright pink and vanilla when Katharina stepped outside. Bernd was still sleeping, and she placed his basket on the bench outside the door, under the eaves. Annamarie squatted on the ground, one of Katharina's wooden clogs in her hand, petting the brown cowhide upper as if it were a pet. Katharina pried it away from her and slid into the shoes, Annamarie jumping up and following at her heels into the yard.

Patches of green grass were exposed between the melting snow in the fields, and the sky was still pink from the dawn. She led Annamarie to the chicken coop and had her scatter the food while she searched one out for soup. The black speckled one was a good pick. She cornered it against the fence and let it do its little jig: left, right, left, right, left, grab! She had her fingers deep in the feathers on its back and swung it into her arms. The chicken clucked nervously, and Katharina soothed and stroked it until it stopped its struggle.

In the yard, she picked up the axe to do away with the head, Hund already near the old tree stump that served as their chopping block. She wiped her brow and looked at the dog, then to where Annamarie was gathering eggs.

Four years ago. It was four years ago since she'd found Angelo's blood trail, had followed it to Karl Spinner's hut.

She lifted the axe over the chicken, surprised by the sudden loss of strength in her arms before bringing it down on the bird's neck. Blood spurted and the body jerked, but she held it down tight.

What had she expected? To see Angelo when they started building the reservoir? And what if she did meet him again?

It had been Opa's idea to rein Angelo in by using blackmail, and she had succumbed to him, written that letter. Mentioned that she had a daughter. It had possibly worked to put some sort of end to the reservoir, but hadn't he figured out that he'd left her pregnant? That he had a child here?

Hund whined, eyeing the chicken head, and Katharina shoved her away with one foot. "Just wait a minute."

She chopped off the feet and dropped them to the dog.

Whatever Angelo knew or did not know, she would never find out because now there was no reason for him to come back here, no reason for her to make his acquaintance again. No reason, then, to ever tell Annamarie about her father. She glanced at her daughter and began to tear out the hen's feathers.

The sound of Florian's footfalls on the gravel startled her, and she turned to watch him go to the fountain to shave. He tipped the mirror that he'd hung near the spout so that he could see himself, oblivious to where she stood.

He never asked. Not even when Jutta had mentioned Angelo's name, Florian never asked anything about Annamarie's father. Katharina was certain that he suspected something *because* he never asked. And he didn't ask again when she brought the news about the dam. She'd gone straight home after her walk with Iris, told Hans about it in the cart on the way, and then he told Florian about the dam and about Hitler's trial in Germany, and the two talked into the night as she put the children to bed.

When she'd come back down, Hans's last words were, "Then there's no need to be talking about me leasing the Thalerhof."

She still did not have the courage to ask Florian whether he'd changed his mind about going to Germany. Since last autumn, they often got into heated discussions about it, stalking around one another like two fighting cats. Then there were the times when Annamarie and she were practising Italian words, and Florian would sometimes cast the girl a dark look, or there would be a disapproving glint in his eye.

Katharina told herself she was imagining these things, and as the silence between them increased, there were days she dreamt of telling her husband everything. While they lay on their sides in bed, she could tell him who Annamarie's father was and why he was. She had formulated the possible words over and over, and each time she would build in how much she loved Florian.

That was where she always stopped, at the point where it sounded all contrived.

And when she imagined what Florian would say, she could picture that disapproving look turning into one of utter disappointment, even disgust. Worst of all, he might ask her if Angelo was the reason she wanted so badly to stay at the Thalerhof, and no matter how hard she tried to deny it in that imagined conversation, she could not seem to muster enough convincing in her own heart.

The secret had grown too big. No thanks to Jutta, it had begun choking them. Angelo Grimani had woven his way back into their lives like a swallowwort, strangling them. Telling Florian all about it now would feel as if she'd been lying to him all this time. Telling her version now would be as futile as cutting back the swallowwort, because it would invade their lives more aggressively than ever. Florian could use a name, a real person, against her or, God forbid, against Annamarie.

She heard her husband yelp, then mutter a curse as he shook his razor. She turned back to the chicken, where Hund had left the feet and was licking at the bloodied stump.

"I said stop that," she scolded the dog.

Florian went back into the house, the mirror swinging from the wooden spigot.

"Mama, eggs," Annamarie said, showing her the little basket. "*Uova*."

"That's right," Katharina said, picking one. "*Uova*. That's Italian. Now, go feed the rabbits, and then we have to get to the barn."

When she was finished hanging up the chicken, she went to the stalls and greeted Hans, who was clearing the sheep stall of manure. She picked up an empty milk tin. Florian was already at Resi, so she moved on to the stall across from him as Annamarie went to find the kittens in the back of the barn.

"Cut yourself shaving earlier?" she asked.

Florian grunted.

"Bad?"

"Razor broke."

"I'll get a new one next time I'm in town."

"No need. Got another one."

Hans must have lent him one. She clenched her stiff hands

before putting salve on them, and heard Florian pick up the tin to weigh and record it before moving to Alma.

"Katharina?"

She looked up. He was half-hidden by the cow.

"I have to bring that rifle into town today."

"No, Florian."

"I have to, Katharina." He gave her a hard look, and she was angry that he was hiding behind the cow to tell her this.

"Fine, Florian. Do what you need to."

"Would you rather I go to jail?"

She shook her head, trying to swallow the tears that were rising in her throat. "I said, do what you need to. But I'm not coming with you."

"Didn't expect you to," he muttered, and disappeared behind Alma's flank.

They worked like that, in stony silence, until they'd made their way down the entire row of stalls. She went to Resi to scratch the cow's ears. That action always comforted Katharina, but now she only felt sad. She remembered when Resi was born, the wolf in the yard, the one she'd shot with Opa's rifle.

She left Resi when Florian passed by, and still avoiding her husband, she pitched fresh hay into the troughs. She was almost finished when Bernd started crying from his basket. By the time she reached him, he was already trying to crawl out. Florian came out to line up the milk tins, face down, back turned. Walking away again.

Katharina led the children into the kitchen and set out their breakfast. Hans came in, hands and beard dripping from his washing, and he took a seat between Bernd and Annamarie. Bernd pushed himself against Hans's arm, reaching for the bread, and Hans broke off a piece for him before filling his bowl with whey.

At the stove, Katharina wanted to ask where Florian was,

when her husband walked in, touched her shoulder, and moved back to the door.

"Come with me," was all he said.

She followed him outside and into the workshop between the house and the stable. This was about the rifle. She braced herself for a fight, deciding there would only be one winner anyway, and it was not going to be she. It was never she.

Florian's carpenter tools were hung neatly on the wall as always, but underneath on the worktable, Katharina recognised her mother's pine chest and, next to that, her father's shaving kit and a sheet of paper. It was the drawing her mother had made of the swallows and the nest, the one Katharina had coloured in so that her father could paint them onto the panels. She looked at Florian, surprised.

"I needed a razor, so I looked for your father's old kit, and I found this," he said, lifting the drawing. "I remember you telling me about this, but I didn't know you still had it."

"I forgot I'd put it in there."

He lowered the sheet of paper and turned to the box. She wrapped her arms around herself. There was something else. He'd found Angelo. He must have. Her heart tumbled against her ribs.

His voice was abnormally loud as he reached behind the chest. "I wanted to surprise you and paint the box, so I emptied it straight away."

When he was facing her again, in both his hands was the bloodstained shirt and, on top of it, the blank cream envelope containing the letter she'd written for Annamarie, or for herself, to make sense of it all. It was still sealed.

Angry tears rose, and the image of her husband swam before her.

Softly, he said, "Sometimes, the answers come without having to ask." He held her things out to her as if they would explode.

She shook her head, refusing to take them from him, and swiped at the first traitor tear. "Jutta told you."

"No, she did not. I'll admit, Katharina, I did ask her, but she wouldn't tell me anything. She said it was not her secret to tell." He looked down, his hands trembling as if the shirt and the letter weighed heavily in them. "I'm ashamed, Katharina."

He was ashamed?

"I pride myself on being a man of my word, but I broke my promise to you." When he looked at her again, he was pleading with her. "Katharina, you don't have to tell me what's in the envelope. I assume it's a letter, maybe to him, but you don't have to tell me. I don't know what makes you so determined to stay on here or so determined to hang on to the past."

How could she explain something she did not understand herself?

He placed the shirt and the letter back on the table before facing her again. "I know you don't want to leave Arlund, and I accept that you do not feel strongly enough about me, about my role in this family, to go to Germany."

She started to protest, but he raised a finger to his lips, and she stared at him in bewilderment. He turned away, and Katharina imagined she was driving him to the final edge, that he would take a tool down and turn against her. Instead, at the end of the workbench, Florian lifted a flat piece of wood, as broad as himself and as high as his middle, and came to stand before her again.

"I wanted to save this until our wedding anniversary, but…"

When he turned the wooden board to expose the other side, Katharina gasped. Florian was holding a sign, a plaque, with fine burnt lettering and design. Upon a mountain landscape, Graun's Head towering in the middle, he had burned in the word *Katharinahof*.

She stared at him in disbelief. This time, the tears came for a different reason, streaming down her face. She lifted it from his hands and held it out in front of her.

"Katharina, I'm going to sell the house in Nuremberg and pay off the bank. We'll get the deed then. I may be listed on it, but this is your farm now."

The relief that washed over her was so violent, she had to shove the sign back at him so that she could brace herself on her thighs.

"Katharina? Are you all right?"

She nodded but could not speak.

He bent towards her, trying to help her up, but she wanted to stay there, to feel the intensity in this change between them. To revel in it.

"You and Bernd *and* Annamarie, you're my family now," her husband was saying. "Katharina, I would do anything to protect all of you, but I need you to make a decision."

"Yes," she gasped, and the tears came for a different reason now.

"No more secrets, Katharina. Please. They're poison. From here on in, we're honest with one another."

"Yes." She straightened, still shaking, still gasping. She looked at the sign again, resting up against her mother's pine chest, and shook her head. Katharinahof.

"Florian," she said, the emotion catching in her throat, "what you've done for me? I don't deserve this."

He lifted her chin and gazed at her. "I chose you, not because you needed someone for Annamarie but because I love you. Now it's your turn to choose." He picked the shirt off the table. The letter fell to the floor with a soft clunk. "You may keep him a secret," Florian said, "and it will keep us as strangers living under the same roof. Or choose to be open with me. Choose to trust me. Maybe even choose to love me."

His face was smooth, expectant, as if he seemed ready to accept either decision from her.

From the house, Katharina heard Annamarie squeal and Hans laugh. She would axe that swallowwort for all it was worth and axe it all the more. All she wanted was to be in this man's arms, to raise her children with him. Here, on the Thalerhof. On the Katharinahof.

She wiped the tears with the back of her hands, and when she saw him clearly again, his eyes were bright, caution and hope pooling together. She gathered the strength to step forward, bringing her face so close to his, their foreheads touched.

"I choose you, Florian," she said steadily. "You. We will always choose you."

12

SAN REMO, LIGURIAN SEA, AUGUST 1924

From the veranda of the Hotel Astoria, Angelo watched the silhouettes of fishing boats come into the San Remo harbour as cats of every colour slithered towards the docks. Along the promenade, lined by umbrella pines, hawkers were slowly putting their wares away, locking up the scent of roasted pine nuts and spun sugar. He watched a harried family of six extracting itself from one of the blue-and-white-striped beach huts, the children all in the same black-and-white bathing costumes, only different sizes. Behind them came the hotel staff, sweeping off sand from the lounge chairs and folding down the umbrellas. A young couple strolled by on the veranda, past the line of potted red geraniums and white oleander, so absorbed in one another that Angelo was certain they were honeymooning.

As the tide came in, each new wave crept a little farther up the shore. He could imagine the water reaching for those abandoned footprints on the beach and exchanging them for remnants from the sea. Behind him, he heard his father coming and took one last look at the beach below before turning to face the Colonel. Many things had been thrown from the depths in these recent months, especially for his father.

The Colonel was already dressed for dinner. He leaned on the balustrade next to Angelo and gazed towards the water.

"Everyone settled in?" Angelo asked.

"Your sisters and your mother are still preening. And Chiara?"

"I imagine she's getting ready as well."

"Good. We have a little time to talk about the hearings."

Angelo sighed. The reason for coming here was to get away from the committee and the journalists, if only for a few days.

"This charade of a family holiday can start when Pietro and Beatrice arrive at the weekend," the Colonel said. "By that time I'll have convinced you to give up this martyrdom you're so keen on accomplishing."

Angelo felt his jaw clench. "In the end, I am the one responsible for the Gleno break. At least in part. You are the other part."

The Colonel straightened. "And you are prepared to step down as minister, Angelo? Is that your intention? People in power remain in power because of the dirty work they had to do to get there. And they remain in power because they have a strategy to implement. But if you want to stage this little battle with me, then you had better keep yourself off the front line, or you will achieve nothing."

Angelo shook his head. "You have your ways. I have mine."

"Pin it on your chief engineer."

Of course his father would suggest that. To hell with him. "Stefano would be ruined. He has a family. Young children."

"Indeed, like you. My men will send him where nobody will recognise him. He'll be rewarded amply enough."

"I need Stefano. He's been my number one man. He grew up in Bolzano. Knows the Tyroleans."

His father scowled. "Then it's time he gets to know the rest of his country."

"And who will Grimani Electrical sacrifice? Barbarasso?"

"He is prepared."

Angelo burst out laughing. "For prison?" Of course his father would shoot his favourite pet if it meant survival.

"Either that, or for a fee. Leave that to me. And as you waste your time reinventing safety standards, I have time to consider how to restore my business. A new name, for example. But, Angelo, mark my words: I will recover, and more than that, I will make sure my interests move forward."

When they heard Marco's voice, they both turned around. Chiara was coming out, holding the boy's hand. She wore a loose black dress, the hem embroidered in soft beige and ochre, and a matching blouse tied squarely at the hip. On her head, she wore a close-fitting black cap, her hair done painstakingly in the latest fashion. The only thing that ruined her evening attire was her expression. Angelo knew the Colonel's presence caused the strain.

The Colonel lowered his voice. "When I'm done, Marco will have something to take over."

"That's my job," Angelo snapped. "I'm his father."

"Of course it is. You see, it's just that with Marco, I have a second chance to do things right. You wouldn't deny me that."

Angelo put an end to the quarrel by swinging his son up onto the sun-washed balustrade. He pointed to the sea, positioning himself between the Colonel and Chiara. "Tomorrow, Marco, we're going to hunt for seashells."

His wife was facing the cable car gliding down from Monte Bignone. "And at the weekend, your grandparents d'Oro will take you up the mountain," she said. "You'll see the whole of the Ligurian Sea from the top. Won't that be fine?"

The Colonel grunted. "You needn't wait until the weekend. *Nonna* and I will take you tomorrow."

Angelo bent towards his son's ear but made sure the Colonel could hear him. "We have three weeks. There's time for everything." He cast his wife a look before addressing his father. "Chiara and I would like to go bathing tomorrow and take Marco to build sandcastles, things a four-year-old should do. If you're intent on preparing yourself for the hearings, please do so, but not with me."

His father checked his pocket watch. "We'll be late for dinner. I'm going to fetch the rest of our party." He jabbed a finger into Angelo's shoulder. "You and I are not finished. Think about what I said. It will not be you, but Stefano who will carry the blame for the Gleno."

When the Colonel was inside, Chiara put a hand on his arm. "What is your father up to now?"

Angelo put Marco down, and he ran along the landing. "Let's just enjoy ourselves, please. I'll go get dressed. Then we'll have dinner and go to the casino, as planned. There are so many people here from Bolzano, my father will be too distracted to bother us."

From her expression, he hadn't convinced her. He might remind her that he'd suggested they go on holiday alone in the first place, but she had insisted that her parents come along, and then his mother had started up. It was not worth arguing about it now. Besides, it would be advantageous to keep the peace.

"How do you find the room?"

"Ample space. Marco and his nanny are set up across the hall from us."

At least he'd have Chiara alone, and he was as nervous as a bachelor about it. When he took her hand, he thought she too might be anxious about the shared bed. The idea pleased him. Despite all that had happened in the past eight months—longer— maybe they still had a chance. He was making the effort to prove his good intentions. Even talked about sacrificing himself and resigning as minister of Civil Engineering. He would have to court her again, like he had the first time, and put everything they'd done to one another behind them. He was prepared to do that if she was. A tall order, though, for a woman who held a grudge against him.

He looked at the incoming tide. If only it would swallow up all his mistakes, all his regrets, and carry them away so far that even he could no longer remember them.

~

The air was still warm and scented by sea, jasmine, frying fish, and olive oil as Angelo and Chiara strolled arm in arm to the casino. Ahead, his sisters gossiped busily, categorising the bachelors they'd seen at dinner between handsome and ugly. It was an activity they were able to do freely now that their mother, who'd complained of her usual headache, had turned in for the night. Then there was the Colonel, visibly annoyed by Angelo's avoidance of the hearings. Each attempt his father made to bring it up again, Angelo made certain to deflect.

On the steps of the Art Nouveau casino, he steered Chiara inside, the feel of her back, her movement beneath his hand, a pleasure. Inside, palm fronds reached for the high glass dome above, as if to get away from the thick tobacco smoke. A plush crimson-and-black carpet in Harlequin print, the movement of which played tricks on the eyes, padded the floor. At one table, a group of people cheered as the croupier paid out bets. At another, the house won and the players slumped into their tuxedos for a brief moment before counting out chips for another shot at luck. Amidst the din of casino-goers was the flash and glitter of evening gowns and polished canes. Angelo heard the swish of cards and the knocking of balls on the roulette wheels, like something caught in the paddle of a steamship.

The Colonel had arranged for their entries and returned with chips for all of them. "I reserved a private poker table. Will you join me, Angelo?"

"Chiara and I will take a *prosecco* at the bar." He turned to his sisters. "The two of you as well?"

His sisters nodded, obviously excited by their first visit and about the freedom they had in their mother's—and soon, their father's—absence.

"I'll take care of the ladies," Angelo added.

His father's displeasure only lasted as long as it took for two men to descend on him. Angelo recognised them from the Fascist meetings, and in the next breath, all three men headed for the back of the casino, finally disappearing behind a gilded mirrored door.

At the bar, Angelo called for the barkeep but froze at the sound of a familiar laugh, a calculated, not merry, tone. He whirled around, saw a flash of royal blue and green on gold—a gown—and a head of dark hair. Gina Conti was standing just ten steps away in the centre of half a dozen men in tuxedos. The pistil of a black-and-white flower.

The notion of fleeing died when Gina's eyes darted to him, a glance that was quick and subtle but seemed to set her mind in motion at the discovery of him there. The general stood next to her, head bent, as if listening to his wife's thoughts.

"Sir? What can I get for you?" the barkeep asked.

Angelo shook his gaze away. His sisters and Chiara were pointed elsewhere. "Four *prosecco*."

"Make that five." Gina's voice just behind him, a little laugh at the end of her request. She was at his left elbow but did not look at him. Instead, she turned casually as if to say something to her party of admirers before resting her eyes on him.

"Minister Grimani, you're here too. Bolzano seems to have completely emptied this August. The Tyroleans might get it into their heads to reclaim the city." She leaned back a little to look past him. "I see your wife is here too. Signora Grimani, a pleasure. I am Gina Conti." She offered Chiara her hand, who took it with obvious distaste.

Angelo's heart flipped. "Signora Conti is General Conti's wife and—"

"I know who you are," Chiara said.

Gina flashed her a smile of acquiescence. "A pleasure to finally meet you in person. And these lovely young ladies, Minister?" She now stepped away from the bar, as if to evaluate merchandise. Angelo took in her gold satin gown upon which were alternating rows of emerald-green deer and sapphire hawks.

He played along. "These are my sisters, Cristina and Francesca."

She took a special interest in Francesca. "You must be the same age as my daughter. Perhaps you know my Filipa?"

"No, Signora."

"Certainly you must. Are you not a member of the youth group?"

Cristina answered, "I am. Francesca has more important things to do."

Francesca elbowed her sister.

"That the Colonel would allow for such a gap in the family," Gina said, sounding amused.

"A gap in what?" Chiara challenged.

"Why, in Fascist engagement, of course."

The barkeep placed five stemmed glasses on the bar, and Angelo checked the mirror above. The general was standing alone.

He handed out the drinks. "*Salute.*"

Gina's was the first to touch his, and Chiara brandished her glass at him.

"Did you not want to play roulette, husband?" she said. "A space has opened up at that table there."

He followed her look, but all he saw was a sea of bodies wading by on the red-and-black carpet, the room swimming all the more for all the mirrors. Just below his left shoulder, he could feel Gina as if she were pressing against him, though she was off to the side.

Francesca, eager to play games or be near the bachelors,

grabbed Chiara's hand. "Hurry, *Zia*. Let's get the table. Angelo still has to pay the barkeep." She tugged his wife away with Cristina on their heels.

When he was alone with Gina, Angelo reached for his wallet while looking for the general in the mirror above the bar. He was not too far from where he'd been before, staring at the back of Angelo's head. Christ. Gina was gazing at Angelo with keen expectation as she took a sip from her glass.

He paid the bill before facing her. "It's been a long time, Gina."

"Indeed, Angelo. We haven't spoken since the disaster."

Did she mean the Gleno Dam or the night at the Laurin?

"It must be a relief to have a break from the press for a while."

"By tomorrow they will be here too."

The idea that Michael Innerhofer could appear made him glance in Chiara's direction.

"You look worried," Gina said. "When are the hearings?"

"October."

"Well, the Colonel will certainly manage, won't he? Just the other day, we saw him at the Laurin." She looked thoughtful. "You must be aware of his efforts to regain support for his ventures."

"If I know my father, he will receive the least of penances. A few Hail Mary's and maybe one Our Father."

Gina lifted her head, an appreciative smile. "And you?"

He scuffed the heel of his shoe on the carpet. "According to the Colonel, I'm to sacrifice a lamb to ask the gods for forgiveness."

She rolled her eyes. "Now, now. Let's not start calling *Il Duce* a god just yet." She leaned in, her smile conspiratorial. "He'd wet himself if he heard that."

He had to smile back, feeling surprisingly at ease. He yearned to have more than this one drink with her. He wanted to just be with her and, at the same time, realised that was exactly what all those men who flocked around Gina Conti wanted. This and more. And he had to wonder whether, like he, they ever got more. He had his doubts. He felt sure they had to settle for titbits like this.

He bent over her, his voice low. "Gina, I want to apologise—"

"Don't." She cast another look at the mirror above them. He did too. The general was gone.

Her mood changed once more, this time to something more intimate, as if they were old friends. "I'm going to have a cigarette, and you will light it. We have a little time before our spouses have had enough. But, Angelo, we will not use that time to revisit what happened between us." She took a step back, her eyes on his. "Besides, I know I am not the first you've left behind."

"But that's not true." He felt a sharp prick at the back of his head and automatically scratched the rise of the scar.

She was busy with her handbag and took out an etched cigarette case, flipped it open, and pulled one out before looking at him again. He reached into his pocket for his lighter, but it was not there, and he remembered the day he'd pretended to receive his war medal from Katharina.

"Not true? Then I must take your word for it." She tapped the end of her cigarette on the bar before holding it to her lips. "Be a gentleman, will you?"

The lighter was in his other pocket. He lit Gina's cigarette.

"Your wife is watching."

In the mirror, he saw Chiara at the roulette table. Even in the half dark, he could see she was anxious.

"You really must keep her close to you. She's your best ally," Gina said.

"But my wife is not prepared to forgive me unless I leave the party. Which may mean resigning from the ministry entirely. If I am to enjoy any sort of reconciliation, then that is what she will ask me to do. She's hoping to achieve that on this holiday."

Gina chuckled. "Quite the dilemma." She waved the cigarette towards the roulette table. "And quite shortsighted of her. It's a reaction of the heart, Angelo. She likely believes that if you are prepared to lie to her about your involvement with the party, then you are able to hide a great many things. Things she may never forgive you for." She dropped her arm below the edge of the bar, and he felt her fingertips brush his thigh. The touch jolted him.

Just as quickly, her hand was back on the bar. She smiled behind her cigarette. "She only suspects. Unless you unmask the evidence, such as your desire for me right now."

Her touch still searing through him, he remembered her: Naked. On the bed. He looked over his shoulder to see whether Chiara had noticed anything, but without the mirror, he was disoriented and could not find her. When he faced Gina again, she had turned her attention to the inside of the casino.

"Gina."

"Go to your wife," she said, looking at him again. "You need her alliance just as much as you need your father's leverage. If the tides turn in the Socialists favour, she is the one who will protect you. As for her demands on you, plead to her sensibilities. Admit that you have made mistakes. Not necessarily what they were, or why you made them, but just that you have. Make yourself vulnerable to her. She may be moved to save your soul." Her smile teased him a little, but her grey eyes were solemn.

"Save my soul?"

"The Gleno is not the only thing you'll have to pay penance for."

She put out her cigarette, and Angelo looked for the men she'd abandoned for him. They had all drifted to a card game, including the general.

Turning back to him, she said in a low voice, "You are far from having beaten the Colonel, Angelo. Do what you must to ensure that you still can. Move cautiously. The web is thick. Remember that."

On the beach the next day, beneath the shade of an umbrella, the whispering waves and the hot sun had put Angelo to sleep. What woke him, he did not know. Perhaps his sisters nearby, for when he looked over at Chiara, she was engrossed in her reading in the chair next to him. She did not notice that he was awake, and his eyes roamed over her lean skin, pale and freckled.

He'd made love to her last night. Aroused by Gina at the casino, it had been easy, at least for him, and he believed that Chiara had also been surprised by a feeling of homecoming. Had they waited much longer, Angelo was sure there would have been nothing to salvage.

Francesca said something he couldn't understand, and Cristina squealed. Laughing, his sisters sprang from their lounging chairs and chased each other into the water, all dark curls and long legs. Angelo laughed, and Chiara bent her paper so that she too could watch the girls. He reached out to touch her, still hungry for lovemaking.

She let him stroke her arm before saying, "Angelo, after this holiday, I'd like it if we could resolve our issues and be a family again."

He nodded.

"You know that I am still trying to forgive you. It would help if you... What I mean is, I need you to do something for me. For us." She was behaving as if she were coaxing him into a narrow space.

Lay yourself open, Gina had said. *Make yourself vulnerable.* "You want me to leave the party."

"Would you?"

He pushed his sunglasses up and looked towards the sea. "It's something we can talk about, but not at this moment. I'm enjoying this day, this peace with you."

By her silence, he read pacification. His thoughts drifted to his conversation with Gina. Everything he had thought to have understood about that woman had been turned upside down on its head last night.

His son's squeal interrupted his thoughts. Near the water, Marco was standing with a green plastic bucket over the Colonel, his legs showing patches of the sugar-fine sand that had stuck to them. The Colonel was in a bathing costume, kneeling and excavating their spot on the beach with his big hands. Angelo had never seen his father like this.

"Would you look at that?"

When she did, Chiara's face read a mixture of amusement and scorn.

"I'm going down there to see what those two are up to."

The Colonel and Marco were too busy to notice him, and as he came closer, Angelo could see they had made a circular pit, as if they were building the moat to a castle before the castle itself. Inside and outside the pit were mounds of sand dotted with pebbles and rocks. The mounds were a mess of shapes and sizes, and if they were to be part of the ramparts, then the Colonel was being lax about the design. The two of them were busy near the middle of the pit, building a wall across the excavation. Marco patted the sand into place, and the Colonel gave instructions.

Marco looked up from his end, his little green pail next to him. "Is it time to pour the water in, *Nonno?*"

"What are you doing?" Angelo asked.

"We're building a dam," Marco said, looking at his grandfather again.

"Are you now? What kind of dam?"

The Colonel pulled back from the wall and stepped out of the pit.

"*Nonno*, what is it called again?"

But Angelo could see it now. The scar on his head throbbed.

"Why the look, Angelo?" the Colonel asked. "Marco should

know what it is we do and how. The sand makes an excellent model."

Angelo pointed to the rocks and pebbles grouped inside. There, the Colonel had been pretty precise after all. It was the Reschen Valley. First, Gorf and Spinn, then more rocks and pebbles for Reschen and Graun. "And those? Those are the villages?"

Marco pointed to a sharp rock, bigger than all the others, sticking straight up out of the sand. "That's a big church. *Nonno* says we have to blow up all the houses and buildings."

That rock. The church in Graun. And there, those three stones, that could be Arlund.

"I'll get the water," Marco cried. He ran to where the sea licked the sand.

Angelo watched his son scoop water into the pail and, when he returned, asked Marco to hand it to him.

"But I want to do it," his son whined.

He pried the handle from his boy's fingers. "You will, but before you begin dumping water on these villages, you need me first. I am the one who has to check the dam structures and approve them. And these houses. Did you evacuate the people?"

Marco shook his head. "There are no people, Papa. They're all gone." He put his hand out for the pail, but Angelo hid it behind his back.

"Are you certain? What will happen to them if you pour water all over them?"

His son dug his toes into the sand.

"Angelo," the Colonel said, "we were having a fine time before you came."

"You're the one who said you want to teach him, so let us teach him. Marco, if you want to learn how this is done"—he looked at the Colonel and then at his son—"then it must be done properly. Before you can have this bucket of water, we need to relocate all of these people and their houses." He set the pail off to the side and reached for the stones of Spinn, then placed them on the mounds on the outside of the reservoir. Marco got to work on the other end, on the village of Reschen.

The Colonel brushed sand off his hands, and Angelo checked to see if he too would help relocate the stone houses, but he simply watched.

"You see, Marco," Angelo said as they worked, "what your grandfather has forgotten is that these people's lives come first, and to relocate them is very expensive."

"What's 'spensive?" Marco asked, letting the stones slip from his hands and randomly onto the mounds.

He went to Marco and led him a few steps towards the water. He picked up a broken shell. "If money were shells, then we'd need lots and lots of them. Imagine you have to walk up and down this beach all day long, collecting shells. You have to give the shells to the people in those houses so they can afford to live. What your grandfather has also forgotten is that we don't have enough shells to do that, so you shouldn't have built a reservoir in the first place."

"What your father forgets is that too few shells is a temporary condition. Always." The Colonel had the pail in his hand. He pointed it towards the sea, where in the distance, large ships were heading to Genoa. "You see them? They're sailing to a place called Industry. And in Industry, they make shells." He held the bucket out for Marco. "There's more shells coming, Marco. Pour the water in."

The boy grabbed the bucket—a happy child—and ran to the pit, dumping the water and then running back to the sea to get more.

Angelo turned away, but Marco called after him.

"Don't you want to watch, Papa?"

The Colonel raised his palms. "It's just a game, Angelo."

Angelo walked away before Marco could pour his third pail

over the model reservoir, the soft splash of water on sand trailing him as he walked back to Chiara, dreading what he had to do.

"What's wrong?" she asked from behind her sunglasses.

"My father. I have to keep an eye on him, Chiara."

"What do you mean?"

"If you go down to the beach, you'll see. He will go after that Reschen Valley reservoir as soon as possible, and it will be much too easy for him to succeed if I am no longer minister."

"But you've put an end to that project."

"Temporarily, Chiara. Mussolini is still very interested. I've only managed to buy some time."

She sat up straight and faced him. "I want peace in my family, Angelo. I cannot and will not deal with your lies and your betrayals. What you did to my father is unforgivable."

"Your father knew what was coming. I never intended to lie to you."

She threw herself back into the chair.

He tried again. "My position requires being a member of the party. I didn't have a choice, and I still don't." He could feel her glare even from behind her shades.

"We always have a choice. You have decided that gaining power over your father is more important than we are. If you want us to be close again, Angelo, then you will have to make a different decision. Either a life with me, or you can leave me—and your son—and go to war against the Colonel. But as long as your father has Mussolini's ear, you can—"

"*I* have Mussolini's ear, Chiara. The directives were initiated by *me*."

He pointed to where the Colonel and Marco were still busy with their sand reservoir. He forced himself to speak gently. "You see that over there? He's teaching Marco how to build dams. I have this reoccurring nightmare, Chiara. Ever since I left the Reschen Valley, it keeps coming to me."

"And?"

"I remember it every time I wake up: I'm standing on a hill above the two lakes. I watch the valley flooding, the water sweeping the villages away, and I feel as if I am losing someone, that there is someone I need to help." He realised he was in danger of revealing too much, and not just to her. It would change everything.

"Your conscience is a funny thing, Angelo. Maybe that someone is me. Have you ever thought of that?"

He had not.

"Why didn't you ever tell me about this nightmare of yours?"

He reached for her hand, and she let him take it. "I don't know. Can we let it be for now?" He squeezed her hand. "I need to stay on as minister, Chiara. And when the hearings are over, I promise everything will be different."

She turned away from him, her hand slipping from his. "So you'll do what the Colonel says and have Stefano take the blame?"

"Maybe I can manage something else." He smiled at her.

Hers, in return, was still cautious but gave him some assurance.

"Let's just leave it now."

When he looked over to where the Colonel and his son were, he was surprised to see that Gina and the general were standing with them. She wasn't looking in their direction, and he wished she would, for Angelo felt a sudden urge to tell Gina how he was succeeding at reconciling with his wife. And maybe Gina would have some ideas about the hearings, about Stefano. About his own political future. He could see that was where things would have to go now.

"Shall we turn in early tonight, Angelo?" Chiara asked. She had her eyes closed next to him.

He glanced back at Gina, who was moving towards the hotel. "I would, darling, but I thought we'd go to the casino again. I've arranged to play poker tonight." It wasn't quite a lie. He still had time to arrange it.

"I don't care to go to the casino again."

"Then wait for me? I won't be long. Promise." He stood up and kissed her cheek just as Gina disappeared from view. "I'll get us some refreshments from the bar."

Chiara's eyes were still closed. "Fetch your sisters out of the sun before you go."

In the hotel lobby, he looked for Gina but did not find her. He asked the clerk for a pen and paper and wrote, *Must see you. Can you get away?* He put it into an envelope and addressed it, his pulse unsteady.

That evening, before dinner, the concierge delivered a note to him. *Hotel's boathouse. 11 p.m. Putting in an appearance at the casino first.*

As would he.

∼

Angelo exchanged his money for chips and jogged up the steps to the hall. Near the second roulette table, his eyes landed on a short dark-haired woman in a black-and-white gown, but it was not Gina. At the invitation of a politician, Angelo went to a poker table in one of the rooms behind the mirrors and made sure to lose the first few hands. After politely taking his leave, he looked for Gina again, but could not find her. She must be already waiting for him at the boathouse.

He hurried back to the Hotel Astoria and out onto the veranda, where he slipped off his Oxfords, then the garters and socks, and stuffed the latter two into the shoes. He carried them down to the boathouse. The wet sand was cool on his soles, though he did not enjoy the murky sponginess of it.

At the door, he knocked, ridiculous as it was, as if Gina might have arranged an earlier meeting with someone else. But nobody was there. Inside, and blinded by the dark, the only relief from the slats in the walls, he felt even more embarrassed. What did he want from Gina? It was Chiara that he was trying to win back.

He stood in the middle of the hut, his only company the smells of briny water and musty life jackets. He thought of all the fights he'd been having since the Gleno, and with it came the remorse for that night at the Laurin with Gina. He should never have taken his frustration out on her. Not like he had. He could have had an ally in her, a friend, and had ruined it with his lust, had revealed the worst of himself to her.

How had it all gotten that far? He thought back to the beginning: meeting Chiara, marrying her, settling down with her family, gaining Pietro's trust and then the job. The instructions and the journey to the Reschen Valley. The lakes. The attack on him by that maniac smuggler.

The girl.

That was where this had all started. She was at the root of all his problems: his reoccurring panic, that nightmare about the lake. She was a whole other world away, so what did she hold over him to make him care so much? He owed her for saving his life, certainly, and the project was probably morally wrong, but he was no longer convinced that the Reschen Valley was worth the greatest conflict between him and the Colonel. Or losing his wife over it.

There was a hollow thud outside. He waited for the door to open, for Gina to call to him, and when that did not happen, listened for more clues. The thudding returned again, pounding with each wave. Someone had not pulled a tread boat far enough up shore.

It had to be long past eleven by now. Maybe she had become distracted, more interested in someone else's cause. He'd been a fool to come here.

He opened the door to a solitary, moonlit beach. He let it fall closed behind him and walked to where he and his family had spent their day. It served Gina right if she arrived now, left to wonder if he'd come at all. Just past the rows of abandoned loungers, he turned and walked backwards, watching for movement near the boathouse. She would see him if she looked.

He stumbled, and a sharp pain ripped through his heel. When he grabbed his foot, the right shoe fell into a shallow pool of water. Cursing, he retrieved it and shook it off, his foot still throbbing. Looking for what had hurt him, he recognised the pit. The Colonel's dam.

The waves had washed most of it away, but there was a dark object in the sand. When he bent over it, Angelo saw the rock Marco had used as the church. St Katharina.

Shame had prevented him from doing many of the right things. All the decisions he had taken since the Reschen Valley had shaped him into nothing he had imagined for himself. Redemption was too far to reach from where he now stood. When he remembered the offer the Colonel had made to relocate Stefano, Angelo laughed. At once he wished he could be one of those men his father was so good at making disappear. Or like that employee of his who'd gone off to America to be, he'd said, far from the eyes of his patriarchs.

He turned to face the boathouse again, but he knew she was not there. Even if Gina had come, he could not have told her any of this. He'd already lied to her. She would only be another person he would disappoint.

He picked up Marco's rock, carried it far from the sea, and set it straight up in the sand. Beneath the hotel's veranda again, he searched out the windows and balcony of his room. The lights were still on.

Chiara, as promised, was waiting for him.

AN EXTRACT FROM BOLZANO

CHAPTER 1
Reschen Valley, April 1937

The grasses were just ankle high as Annamarie ran through the meadow. Her mother's last words, *You're a young woman—behave like one*, dispersed on the spring wind.

Being a young lady meant no longer playing house but *keeping* house. It meant everyone else had only one plan for her future, one wrought in tradition and old-fashioned beliefs. And a man. Another farmer.

She imagined her family discovering that she'd fled the *Hof* again. Mother would smell the scorched milk, find the kitchen empty, and move to the doorway, the ends of her headscarf flapping like a frantic truce flag in the *Föhn*. She would ask Bernd, as he pitched manure, if he'd seen his older sister, and Bernd would complain that Annamarie had again shirked her chores to find escape in running. Manuel could look up from the garden and still see her.

"Annamarie," her baby brother might call. "Wait for me."

She waited for no one. She had no time to wait. Her father,

cleaning out the milk pails, would hear of it, and he would be resigned. "She's sixteen," she imagined him saying, as if that should explain his position on things. That thought made her laugh, and every impact with the spongy ground created a gasp, a sound not unlike sobbing.

Yes, she was sixteen, and she was running because she still could.

Down the back road leading from Arlund to the valley below, she anticipated the tree roots, her arms outstretched with each hazardous leap. At the wayward crucifix, she stopped long enough to make the sign of the cross. Graun's Head, the peak that marked where their summer alp was, was still covered with snow, and as she continued to run down the road, she felt the rest of the alpine mountains closing over her. On the valley floor, the lakes shimmered in the spring sun, still crusted with ice and snow on the shady sides. The air was warmer when she reached the bottom of the road, and she slowed as she passed the police quarters, where none of the *carabinieri* paid much attention to another milkmaid. As long as she did not run, they did not whistle or shout, "Where are you off to, *fidanzata?*"

On the road between the two towns, she turned left towards Graun and slipped past the bank, then the seamstress, where Annamarie ought to later be for her home economics session. She ducked her head when she saw *Podestà* Rioba. He and the balding *segretario* nailed a banner onto the front of the town hall.

She slowed down to read it: *Mussolini ha sempre ragione.* Mussolini is always right.

Why did they have to hang up a sign to remind them? Il Duce, she'd learned in school, was not to be disputed in anything.

When she moved on, she decided the banner was for the "others." Just like the signs in every authority's office: *We speak*

Italian. Or the one above the classroom blackboard: *It is forbidden to spit on the floor and to speak German.* The other day, she saw Jutta Hanny get a two thousand lire fine because she'd written *Welcome to South Tyrol* on the front of her inn. And then, even worse, underneath: *No Walscher,* the derogatory name for the Italians. All this in German! Someone had really made her angry for her to have gone so far.

Annamarie was just outside the Foglios' butcher shop when Sebastiano Foglio came out with a loop of smoked sausage in his hand.

"Where you going, Annamarie? To the Planggers' tree?"

"Maybe." Where else was there to go but to the Planggers' tree?

"I'll join you."

"I might just go for a walk."

"Suit yourself." He went back inside but was untying his smeared apron. The smells of garlic and smoke drifted out behind him.

The bakery was right down the street, and Annamarie went in, keeping her eye on the road through the window, watching for Sebastiano.

Frau Prieth waddled out of the back and stood behind the baked-goods counter. "*Griaß-di,*" she said in the Tyrolean dialect. "*Was hosch,* Annamarie Steinhauser?" What have you got?

She cast a look at Annamarie's feet, and Annamarie wiped her boots on the mat.

Annamarie had but one coin, and as Sebastiano passed the shop, she turned her back to the door and faced the glass case. The *Gipfel,* filled with hazelnut paste, were lined up in even rows. "I'll take one of those, please." Annamarie heavily accented her German to sound like an Italian.

The baker's wife wrapped the pastry in silence, her mouth turned down. With the *Gipfel* in her smock, Annamarie stepped outside again, guessing that Sebastiano had taken the direct way to the Planggers' tree.

～

It was chilly in the crook of the branch, and they did not take off their boots to hang bare feet over the creek. A lone frog croaked in the nearby pond. Annamarie's scalp itched from the tight braids her mother had made, but she could not unbraid them in front of Sebastiano, lest he believe she'd changed her mind about him.

She unpacked the *Gipfel* and offered him a piece. He took it and looked encouraged, so she moved away before biting into hers.

"Did she talk to you in dialect again?" he asked before tasting his.

Annamarie shrugged. Frau Prieth always talked in their German dialect, just like all Tyrolean children were made to do at home. Most of them anyway. Sebastiano was one of those few who didn't have to.

"Go ahead. Talk like your father with his high German accent," Sebastiano said. His tone was polite, not taunting like their other classmates', who only wanted her to make them laugh.

Annamarie cleared her throat before taking on her father's crisp Nuremberg accent. She was good at mimicking people. "*Guten Tag*, Frau Prieth. I would very much like a *Gipfel*, if you would be so kind as to oblige me."

Sebastiano laughed and nodded, as if they shared much in common. They didn't. She might sometimes be made fun of because her father spoke the high German, but Sebastiano's family were worse off. The Foglios never spoke the local dialect, had even changed their Tyrolean names to Italian ones. On a bad day, both the Tyrolean and Italian classmates teased Sebastiano. The other day in the schoolyard, where they set up their own courthouse, they'd tried and punished Sebastiano for his father's argument with a Tyrolean farmer, something about an unfair price for the farmer's butchered steer. When the bigger boys dragged and dumped Sebastiano into a container of manure, nobody had helped him out.

"I'm sorry about what happened the other day," she said.

Sebastiano looked cautious. "It was the others who started it."

"My father said I shouldn't listen to what the parents say behind each other's backs."

He finished his pastry and brushed his hands as if the matter was finished and looked towards the lake. Her confession seemed to have caused him to lose his courage. Like last time. When he'd tried to kiss her at the Christmas dance, she'd turned her head so that his mouth landed on her hair.

"I don't want to be a butcher's wife," she'd shouted over the music, though she'd wanted to be kissed.

He'd taken a step back, so when he turned to her once more, she knew she would let him this time, but instead he shouted back, "What do you want to be then?"

"Nothing that has to do with staying here," she'd said.

She told no one what she really wanted. It was her secret. But after Christmas she'd vowed to only unbraid her hair for an Italian boy, declare her love to one who lived far away from here. Then she'd leave with him and cut her hair short like the women in the cities did.

Sebastiano said, "Look at all those cars," breaking into her thoughts.

He pointed across the fields and over Reschen Lake. Three black vehicles had arrived at the military post, and the *carabinieri* were already leaning in at the window of the first one.

"More fortification for the border?" Annamarie asked.

He shook his head. "Soldiers don't arrive in cars. Father said something about electrical-company men coming."

She frowned. Were there problems with the generators?

He swung down from the crook of the tree. "They're from Bolzano, and some are staying at Jutta Hanny's inn. There's so many of them, the Il Dante is full."

Annamarie stared at the cars. From the city!

Only when Sebastiano touched the toe of her boot did she notice him again. "Are you coming then?" he asked. "Father will tan my hide if I don't get back to the shop."

She nodded. She was not going home though. Going by the inn was better than facing her affronted family.

A GUIDE TO THE RESCHEN VALLEY

You can learn about why I wrote this series, what got me started, and even some history around the Oberer Vinschgau Valley, the valley depicted in Reschen Valley.

For historical background pieces, a list of characters in the series, maps and a glossary, visit www.inktreks.com.

Please do consider leaving a book review on Goodreads, Amazon, Bookbub, or any of your other favorite platforms and share them with social media. Your opinion *does* count.

THE RESCHEN VALLEY SERIES

1 | NO MAN'S LAND

A plan to flood a valley. A means to destroy a culture.

It's 1920. The end of the Great War has taken more than Katharina Thaler's beloved family; it has robbed the Austrian Tyrol of its autonomy and severed it in half. As her grandfather's last living relative, Katharina also faces becoming the first woman to own a farm in the Reschen Valley. While her countrymen fight to prevent the annexation to Italy, Katharina stumbles on a wounded Italian engineer on her mountain. Her decision to save Angelo Grimani's life thrusts both into a labyrinth of corruption, prejudice, and greed. Trapped between a new world order and the man who threatens to seize her land, Katharina must decide what to protect: love or country? *No Man's Land* is the first book in the Reschen Valley series.

2 | THE BREACH

Burying the past comes at a high price...

It's 1922 and a year after the Italian Fascists marched on Bozen.

Nationalism in the Tyrolean Reschen Valley creates enemies out of old friends and Katharina Steinhauser fiercely protects the identity of her daughter's father from both her family and her community. Meanwhile, the Fascists have wrested control from the monarchy and momentum behind the Reschen Lake reservoir increases with plans to wipe out the Reschen Valley's towns and hamlets. Katharina risks writing to Angelo Grimani, the man in charge, and begs to have the project reassessed. But Angelo is hemmed in by a force that steers him far from his dealings with the Reschen Valley and that which binds him to Katharina. It's the opportunity the Fascists have been waiting for.

3 | BOLZANO

In the process of understanding who you are, more often you discover who you are not.

1937. Northern Italy. New international conflicts loom on the horizon, and Italy must feed its war machine. Angelo Grimani has a plan to keep the Reschen Valley reservoir out of his father's hands but he needs a local front to succeed. He faces his past and seeks an alliance with Katharina Steinhauser.

Meanwhile, Annamarie Steinhauser is convinced her future lies beyond the confines of the valley. When an Italian delegation arrives to assess the reservoir, Annamarie believes she has found her ticket out…in the form of Angelo's son and a Fascist uniform.

Love, betrayal, and deception explode in the third installment of the Reschen Valley.

4 | TWO FATHERLANDS

How do you take a stand when the enemies lurk within your own home?

1938. South Tyrol. Katharina, Angelo, and Annamarie are confronted by the oppressive force created by Mussolini's and Hitler's political union. Angelo puts aside his prejudices and seeks an alliance with old enemies; Katharina fights to keep her family together as the valley is forced to choose between Italian and German nationhood, and Annamarie finds herself in the thick of a fascist regime she thought she understood. All will be forced to choose sides and none will escape betrayal.

Releases April 13, 2021! Order now!

Early readers are calling this "…gripping, taut, packed with moral dilemmas, and nail-biting twists!"

5 | THE RISING

A homecoming like no other.

June 11 1961. Explosions rock South Tyrol as pylons and electric masts are toppled by members of the South Tyrolean Freedom party's underground. Annamarie Steinhauser-Greil's documentary and reports on the flooding of the Reschen Valley some twelve years earlier are used in the defense of her brother, Manuel, who is facing a death sentence if found guilty of taking part in the terrorist act. But when Annamarie returns to the valley to prepare for her testimony, she must wrestle with what has become of the family she left behind, and the past that lies beneath the Reschen Lake reservoir.

Coming in 2022!

0 | THE SMUGGLER OF RESCHEN PASS: THE PREQUEL

Pride comes before the fall.

1900s Austrian Tyrol. Fritz Hanny, confident and optimistic, enjoys the prestige of belonging to one of the most respected families in the Reschen Valley. When he falls in love with Cecilia, a young girl in a neighboring village, he is certain he has found his purpose in life. Already on his way to making his own fortune, Fritz pursues Cecilia only to be cut down by one external force after another. Disappointment, violence, and conflict turn Fritz into a desperate man.

"Lucyk-Berger has explored the darker side of human nature in this tale, and she has done so with great skill and splendour. This story appalled, impressed, and fascinated in equal measures. It is wonderfully told and impossible to put down." - Mary Anne Yarde, Coffee Pot Book Club blogger

For a guide to this series, including historical notes, maps, glossaries and articles, visit **www.inktreks.com**.

ACKNOWLEDGMENTS

Thank you, Dori Harrell, for once again helping me to sing in key! I especially wish to thank Antonio Aivan for his help with the northern Italian translations and to the great WIP Team at the Faber Academy for your continued support, especially Ilona Bannister and Fiona Egglestone. To my ARC team, you're awesome!

ABOUT THE AUTHOR

CHRYSTYNA LUCYK-BERGER is an award-winning American author. She travels for inspiration and is inspired by what she encounters. She lives in Austria in her "Grizzly Adams" mountain hut with her hero-husband, hilarious dog, and cantankerous cat.

Her Reschen Valley series, which takes readers to the interwar period of northern Italy's Tyrolean province, has been hailed as "wonderful historical fiction," and "a must read." Her World War 2 novels have garnered awards and recognition. You can find all her works on her website, Goodreads, Bookbub, Facebook, Instagram and Twitter.

Author Homepage
www.inktreks.com

Subscribe to get news from behind-the-scenes, historical backgrounds from upcoming projects and inspiring author interviews from the historical fiction genre.

Dear Reader, your reviews matter.
Please be so kind to consider sharing your impressions with other potential fans. Or if you were not thrilled with this book—if it did not broaden horizons, surprise you with new insights, or

move you—feel free to reach out and let me know how I might do better.

Yours,
   Chrystyna

~

ALSO BY CHRYSTYNA LUCYK-BERGER

The Smuggler of Reschen Pass: A Reschen Valley Novella

Prequel to the series and a stand-alone psychological thriller

Reschen Valley 1: No Man's Land

A plan to flood her valley. A means to destroy their culture.

The first book in the award-winning series about a woman who fights for her homeland when an oppressive Italian government moves to eradicate her valley's Tyrolean identity and wipe it off the map.

Reschen Valley 2: The Breach

Burying the past comes at a high price.

Reschen Valley Box Set: Season 1 – 1920-1924

She wants her home. He wants control. The Fascists want both. Contains books 1 and 2 and *The Smuggler of Reschen Pass.*

Reschen Valley 3: Bolzano

On the journey to figuring out who you are, most often you discover who you are not.

Reschen Valley 4: Two Fatherlands

How do you take a stand when the enemy lurks where you thought was safest?

Reschen Valley Box Set: Season 2 – 1937-1949

Sometimes, when you're trying to determine who you are, what you discover is who you are not. Contains books 3 and 4.

Reschen Valley 5: The Rising (2024)

A homecoming like no other.

∽

Souvenirs from Kyiv

Unforgettable stories based on the heartbreaking experiences of
Ukrainian families during WW2

∽

The Girl from the Mountains

Not all battles are fought by soldiers.

The Woman at the Gates

They took her country. But they will never take her courage.

And stay tuned for more books published by Bookouture, Hachette UK

Printed in Great Britain
by Amazon